THE MYSTERIOUS ENCOUNTERS
OF JOSEPH TROPEA

THE MYSTERIOUS ENCOUNTERS OF
JOSEPH TROPEA

Anthony J. Vartuli

SOJOURN WAY ministries

sojournwayministries.org

Published 2025 by PilgrimWay Books,

Scripture quotations labeled ESV are from, The Holy Bible, English Standard Version® (ESV®), copyright © 2001 by Crossway, a publishing ministry of Good News Publishers. Used by permission. All rights reserved. ESV Text Edition: 2007.

Scripture quotations marked NIV are taken from the Holy Bible, New International Version®, NIV®. Copyright © 1973, 1978, 1984, 2011 by Biblica, Inc.™ Used by permission of Zondervan. All rights reserved worldwide. www.zondervan.com The "NIV" and "New International Version" are trademarks registered in the United States Patent and Trademark Office by Biblica, Inc.™

Scripture quotations labeled NLT are from the *Holy Bible*, New Living Translation, copyright © 1996, 2004, 2007 by Tyndale House Foundation. Used by permission of Tyndale House Publishers, Inc., Carol Stream, Illinois 60188. All rights reserved.

Verse from the Song "This is your Land" by Phil Baggaley, David Clifton, and Ian Blythe is from their album *City of Gold*. Permission to use this verse was given by Toms Hays, IQ Music Publishing.

The hymn, "Holy, Holy, Holy" was written by Anglican bishop Reginald Heber and was first published posthumously in 1826.

Inspiration for *The Last Door* came from a painting by a dear friend, Vaila Backhouse.

The candelabra on the book cover comes from an actual candelabra that I own. I tried to find the original artist but he/she could not be found.

Library of Congress Control Number: 2025915674

ISBN: 979-8-218-74482-3

For the small group I journey with:

Diane Vartuli, Brenda Miller,
Freddy and Sarah Feliciano, Duncan and Angie Sprague,
Brian and Jean Fast, Kep and Kimmie Crabb

*I'm deeply grateful for an environment of safety where we can
be our flawed selves, where relational wisdom is offered in
such a way that it releases God's life from
within us toward others.*

These things – the beauty, the memory of our own past – are good images of what we really desire; but if they are mistaken for the thing itself, they turn into dumb idols, breaking the hearts of their worshippers. For they are not the thing itself; they are only the scent of a flower we have not found, the echo of a tune we have not heard, news from a country we have never yet visited.

C.S. Lewis

These all died in faith, not having received the things promised, but having seen them and greeted them from afar, and having acknowledged that they were strangers and exiles on the earth. For people who speak thus make it clear that they are seeking a homeland. If they had been thinking of that land from which they had gone out, they would have had opportunity to return. But as it is, they desire a better country, that is, a heavenly one. Therefore God is not ashamed to be called their God, for he has prepared for them a city.

Hebrews 11:13–16

CONTENTS

FOREWORD

KEP CRABB, FOUNDER AND DIRECTOR OF
LARGERSTORY MINISTRIES

Some books entertain us, some inform us, but a rare few invite us to face the deepest realities of our lives as it comes to an end. *The Mysterious Encounters of Joseph Tropea* is such a book. In these pages, Anthony Vartuli offers more than a story—he shows us a journey to the end of hope, faith, and the mystery of what lies beyond the veil of this life.

Joseph Tropea is not simply an imagined figure moving through the final days of life. He is a character shaped by Anthony's years of walking beside the dying in hospice care, where suffering, tenderness, fear, and grace often meet in ways never experienced before. Because of that lived experience, Joseph's journey feels honest and deeply human. As he slowly moves from this world to the next, we witness not only the frailty of the body, but also the awakening of the soul.

This story confronts the truth that none of us can escape: one day, each of us will face our own dying. Yet rather than leaving us in dread, this book asks a better question, *how will we embrace that day when it comes?*

In Joseph's mysterious encounters, there is an extraordinary paradox: even in the midst of dying, he has never felt more alive. That paradox gives this book its quiet power. It reminds us that life is brief, eternity is real, and the way we finish this race called life matters as much as the way we began this journey.

As you read these pages, I believe you will find yourself reflecting not only on Joseph Tropea's life ending on this side, but also on your own story as we move to the end of this journey. You may come away asking how you wish to live, how you wish to love, and how you hope to enter eternal life. My hope is that this book will stir in every reader the same desire it stirs in me: to meet that final passage with the faith, courage, and love that Joseph Tropea so movingly reveals. Anthony Vartuli has given us a story that is both sobering and full of hope that lingers in the heart long after the final page.

NOTE TO THE READER

This story is a work of fiction. I don't claim to fully understand what heaven might look like (although we do get some glimpses in the Bible). Nor do I claim to know how the dying interact with the unseen world (although some personal testimonies from those in the dying process have caused me to be curious). In my work as a hospice chaplain, I have sat with many who are on the threshold of this world and the next. It is a most sacred place for those who are opening their very lives to God. Even for those who remain closed to God, it is sacred. For the latter, it is a sacred opportunity missed or, to put it another way, a sacred opportunity rejected. Yet, I don't always know who is doing the receiving or the rejecting. Dying, among many other things, is a very mysterious process. As in all aspects of life, God's mysterious work must be entered as opposed to dispelled. When we enter mystery, it has the potential to produce a bit more humility in us. At least that has been my experience.

One of my goals in writing this book was to stir up what

Eugene Peterson called a "biblically informed imagination" (*Christ Plays in Ten Thousand Places*) so the truths of the Bible might come alive to us in new and thought-provoking ways.

Another guiding thought as I wrote the book came from C. S. Lewis who said that God means to get us as far along as possible before death, as far along in the sanctification process, in the becoming-relationally-holy process (*Mere Christianity*). I love that thought, but if I am to be honest, I don't always like it, especially when I am suffering.

As a work of fiction, none of the characters in this book represent any real life person. If for some reason you might be reminded of someone you know, or reminded of yourself, it is either purely coincidental, or perhaps the Holy Spirit is putting his finger on something important concerning the life of someone you may know or concerning your own life. In either case, it would be good to ponder where and how God might be leading you. It has been my desire and prayer that he may, in fact, do so.

I have used the vehicle of story to hopefully introduce you, the reader, to what I understand to be relational theology, which has also been called spiritual theology. Larry Crabb once said that relational theology develops as the Holy Spirit weaves systematic theology and biblical theology into a story, the relational story that God is telling (*A Different Kind of Happiness*).

While the fictional story of this novel can be debated, the relational truths I have attempted to introduce emerge from the Bible. They don't belong to me, nor do they belong to any other saint/sinner for that matter. They belong to the Father, Son, and Holy Spirit. All of God's relational truths are rich and profound, some simple and some more difficult to understand. Yet, all of them are worth knowing and pondering. God's truths are not meant to just be heady but are meant to make their way deeply into our minds and hearts. They are meant to profoundly change the way we relate to God, to others, and even to ourselves. It is my hope and prayer that through this story a few of God's relational truths might do that very thing, begin to seep way down deep. Since God's deepest state of being is relational as Father, Son, and Holy Spirit, I ultimately trust that he will get his relational work done in you . . . and also in me. Should he use this novel to help inch some of us down the salvation road, I would be immensely grateful.

I do hope the story will draw you to God in some way, but if you are also disrupted by some of what you read in this novel, believe me, you are in good company. I, too, have been disrupted and continue to be disrupted by God's relational truths. It is not by mistake that the Word of God is likened to a two-edged sword (Hebrews 4:12). Soul surgery is often needed before soul healing can take place. However you are being led I trust that, like Jacob, who wrestled with God all night, this story will give you permission to do the same. God honors such wrestling. I believe it is the only way to know the Father, Son, and Holy Spirit better.

- Anthony J. Vartuli

ONE
THE LOOMING DARKNESS

In order to arrive at what you are not
you must go through the way in which you are not.
And what you do not know is the only thing you know...
- T. S. Eliot, Four Quartets

All fears are rooted in the fear of death. These words penetrated the mind of Joseph Rafael Tropea as he lay still in his hospital bed at Bright Star nursing home in rural North Carolina, incrementally paralyzed by the devastating effects of Multiple System Atrophy, a disease that now rendered his body almost as useless as a burned-out toaster while leaving his agile mind lucid as a chess player thinking several moves ahead.

Why this phrase? Why is it surfacing now? As he searched his memory banks, Joe's mind wandered back in time. He pictured the person who first uttered those words to him.

It was that homeless man, living on the streets of Manhattan. Yes, I remember now! He was in a tattered overcoat. His basketball sneakers were threadbare. I was a young Christian, working with that inner city ministry, passing out gospel tracts to people living on the streets. What was the name of that ministry? It's hard to remember. Anyway, that's when he came up to me, that man dressed in rags. He took the tract out of my hand, grabbed my coat, and pulled me close. Our faces were just inches apart. Joe gagged as he recalled the stench of grime mixed with alcohol on the man's breath.

Tears were running down his face. There was compassion in his dark green eyes. Those eyes, so penetrating! It was at that point he spoke those words to me, "All fears are rooted in the fear of death." He spoke urgently, as if my life depended on hearing those words. When it was obvious I had no response, he let go of me. Yes, that's right. Now I remember. He let go. Then he turned his back to me and briskly walked away. I never saw him again.

The recollection of the homeless man was so powerful Joe's heart pounded as if it might beat out of his chest. Nevertheless those words remained etched in his mind, calling out to some deep reality within his soul. Deep calling out to deep. Forever changing his outlook on life.

Can life truly be lived, fully lived, without facing one's own impending death? His Socratic mind was whirling, asking questions which were not easily answered. With his heart pounding and his thoughts racing, he brooded over these words as if searching for an answer that could somehow set his trapped soul free from his withering body.

As his mind quickened in pace, another question surfaced. *Who was it who once said that the present moment is where time touches upon eternity?* His thoughts stretched again like a rubber band about to snap.

As a retired philosophy teacher, questions like these were not unusual for him. Good questions, he understood, didn't exist for themselves. They were meant to lead somewhere, into a more spacious life, into a more comprehensive understanding of oneself, into a deeper relationship with God.

Yet, now his teacher's mind, like an unhinged carousel, was spinning out of control. The questions were coming faster and faster, and he didn't know how to stop them. He was a bird in a cage longing to be free. The only thing that seemed to be working was his mind. Yet now, even his mind was betraying him. The edges of his thoughts were fraying, unraveling like a loose ball of twine. All seemed to be lost, and a darkness enveloped him like a black cloud, a darkness he had never experienced before.

My God, my God, why have you forsaken me? In despondency, he voiced the words of Jesus as he hung on the cross, hoping to find some comfort in the utterance. But no such comfort came.

"God, are you real?" he asked aloud as if God's reality was but a mere shadow of days gone by, a lie he once bought into for personal comfort. His body and soul ached like that of a wounded soldier in a foxhole for a sense of God's reassuring presence. Now, as an octogenarian coming to grips with the special gift of each living breath, it was even more clear that he was not in charge of the times when God made his presence known. Yet, knowing this only made things more difficult. He was at the mercy of a God who at times seemed entirely unreasonable, even crazy.

God, I need to experience you! I want to experience you

right now! As those words went through his mind, he knew they did not come from a place of surrender. They came from an internal demand. He was desperate, and a demand seemed reasonable. Yet, while Joe's demand to experience God on his own terms was very real, there was also a deeper yearning in his soul for something that his demanding spirit could never deliver.

As much as Joe wanted to feel the reassuring presence of God, he wanted much, much more. Deep down, he wanted God *himself*. He wanted the *living* God. The God who could not be controlled or manipulated and yet was for him in the deepest way. The God who was both solid and loving, unpredictable and kind. The God who could give his all for the sake of others and still remain at the center of all things. The God who, at times, withdrew a sense of his presence to accomplish something deeper. The God who longed to redeem all that was so deeply flawed within him and have a good time doing it. The God so full of grace that no amount of sin could cause him to retreat.

In this moment, however, his demand overshadowed his deeper desire. It was his fear that was winning the day. With his whole body trembling and his mind on the edge of delirium, Joe's hands searched for the bedrails on each side of the hospital bed. It was difficult because they were always in the down position (his bed was also low to the ground with a cushioned mat beside it in case he fell to the floor).

When his hands finally found the bedrails he grabbed them and let out a scream so loud it could be heard throughout the entire nursing home. Joe could faintly hear someone running down the hallway just outside his room. Suddenly there was a figure of a person who came and knelt beside his hospital bed. Someone was trying to talk to him. It was a woman's voice.

"Joe. Joe! Hey! It's Dalia! Joe, remember me? I met you last week. Come on now. It's OK. It's OK. You're all right. I'm right here. I'm with you now." He could feel her warm hands gently cupping his cheeks.

"Breathe in through your nose and out through your mouth. Do it with me, Joe. We'll do it together. Smell the roses. Deep breath in. Blow out the candles. Deep breath out. Yes, that's it. Now let's do it again. Deep breath in. Yes, good. And now deep breath out. That's wonderful, Joe. You're doing great."

He was listening to her and doing his best to breathe as she had instructed.

They continued this breathing exercise on and off for twenty minutes until Joe slowly regained equilibrium. His heart rate slowed, and his breathing returned to a more rhythmic pace. Joe opened his eyes and saw her, Dalia, a thirty-five-year-old Black woman, who happened to be Joe's hospice CNA.

Letting out a deep sigh, he said, "Oh, it's you! Thank God it's you! Dalia, right? Thank God! I was in such a dark place. It seems I'm falling apart little by little. I've never felt so . . . so . . ."

Dalia waited and then said, "Go on."

"Forgotten, abandoned."

Stuttering a bit, Dalia said, "Oh . . . I mean . . . really?"

"It's as though my whole being is unraveling, at times lost in a darkness I've never known before. When I'm shrouded in darkness, certain questions assault me."

"Questions?"

"Yes, questions. Irrational questions but they're real nonetheless."

"What kind of questions?"

"Have I really accomplished anything good? Have I ever impacted anyone for the good? Have I ever truly revealed God to my children, my grandchildren? Has anyone noticed the life of God in me? Have I been abandoned by . . . by . . ." His voice trailed off.

"By who?"

"By God himself."

Dalia, looking somewhat shocked, said, "That sounds terrible."

"Terrible does not even begin to describe it."

"How are you doing now?

"Better, now that I am talking to you. I think it's the silence that sometimes triggers it, the darkness. Not sure."

"I'm so sorry you're going through this, Joe."

He could see that she felt a bit helpless.

Fumbling with her words, she said, "Can I . . . I mean is there anything I can do for you? What can I . . . rather . . . how can I make you more comfortable?"

"I honestly don't know," Joe said, his head bobbing slightly and his eyes still trying to focus.

"Look at me, Dalia," he continued. "This body is wasting away. I have my mind, I can still speak, although that's also becoming more difficult. It's tough. It's really, really tough."

With moist eyes, Dalia smiled and reached into her bag. Fidgeting around, she grabbed hold of something. "I know it's not much, but maybe this will help a little?" She pulled out a diffuser, set it on the night stand, and plugged it in. She took a cup to the sink and filled it with water and gingerly poured the water into the diffuser. Then she reached in her bag and pulled out some scented oils: cinnamon, lemon, eucalyptus, tea tree, lavender. She showed them to Joe. "Should we give this a try, Joe? If so, is there any particular oil you prefer?"

He smiled in appreciation. "Why don't we try eucalyptus?"

"Sounds like a plan." Dalia lifted off the top and put a few droplets in the diffuser. Then she switched it on. Gradually the scented fragrance enveloped the room. Joe fully let go of the bed rails, and his body began to relax.

He saw her look out of the corner her eye. Dalia happened to notice a picture hanging on the wall near the bay window in his room. She went over to look at it. "Who's this, Joe?"

"Oh, that's Maria."

Dalia remained quiet.

"She was my wife. She died ten years ago of stage four breast cancer. It's an old picture, Maria was in her late twenties when it was taken."

Dalia gazed at the picture.

"We were on a hike in Utah. She was in front of me on the trail. She looked back at me and smiled. That's when I took the picture."

"She's beautiful. Her long brown hair is stunning."

"She was beautiful body and soul." There was a pause. Then Joe's voice lowered. "It was all rather quick. Two months from diagnosis to death. We barely had enough time to say goodbye. Even though I know I'll see her again, it's rough being here without her. I always thought I would be the first to go. Ya know? We enjoyed a good marriage. Sure, we had our difficult seasons, but all in all it was rich and beautiful. *She* was beautiful." There was a joy and heaviness to his words.

"I can only imagine that made the parting all the more difficult."

"Yes. It sure did," He said, fighting back the tears.

They sat in silence once more.

"Thanks for sharing that with me. I really appreciate it."

"Thanks for listening, Dalia. That's a rare quality."

"I suppose you're right," she said thoughtfully.

After a little while she asked, "You mentioned your kids? Do you get to see them at all?"

"I used to see them quite often. My son, Patrick, and his wife, Sonya, live in Arizona. My daughter, Anna, is married to Sam. They live in New Hampshire. We are pretty spread apart. After Maria died, we made it a point to get together at least twice a year. Our gatherings normally took place here, in North Carolina."

"Grandkids?"

"Yes. I have three. Patrick has two kids, a boy and a girl. Anna has one girl."

"I bet they are the joy of your life."

"You guessed it. Yet, since I was diagnosed with MSA it's become harder and harder to see them. I decided to live here at Bright Star. It was getting too difficult to stay in my home. Plus all the memories of Maria. It just became too hard over time. There's really nothing I can do with my grandkids here given my condition. Plus, I don't like them seeing me this way, so useless. God knows how much I miss them." His loneliness stung him, like a swarm of angry bees, as he said those words.

"Patrick and Anna stay in touch with me. I'm blessed to have fantastic kids. They're always calling me just to make sure I'm okay. I just don't want to burden them too much. Ya know what I mean? They have their own lives to live. I know it's rough for them as well, to see their dad being reduced to . . . to . . ."

"To what?"

"To a helpless old man."

Dalia slightly frowned as she scratched her head with her forefinger.

Joe could see that she was struggling to find something positive to say.

"It sounds like you have been a good dad to them. Yes?"

"I hope so. I truly do. I wonder sometimes. I have tried to reveal Jesus to them. More than anything, I want them to experience Jesus through my life."

Dalia appeared uncomfortably quiet.

Sensing an awkwardness between them, Joe changed the subject. "Well, look at me. I've done all the talking and you all the listening. I'd love to hear about your family at some point. You don't have to share Dalia. No pressure. Just invitation."

"I would love to share. Maybe not today though. You need rest. Let's save it for another time when you're feeling better. I'll leave the diffuser on for you. I can even leave the scented oils so the caregivers at the facility can refill it. That sound okay?"

Not wanting to push, Joe said, "That's kind of you, thanks. Your coming today could not have been more timely. And the diffuser has helped to calm me down some."

"It's my pleasure. It's Thursday today. How about I plan on coming back on Tuesday of next week? How does that work?"

"Sounds great. Thanks so much."

"You get some rest now. I hope you don't have any more of those nightmares."

"That makes two of us."

With that, Dalia gathered her things and slipped out the door.

A few hours went by. It was Thursday afternoon. The room was quiet for the most part, except when facility staff came in to check on him, change him, offer him very small bites of food which proved difficult to eat, dispense his medications, and refill the diffuser when desired. Both Patrick and Anna called that evening, which brought a combination of pain and gladness to his heart.

At times, he was aware of a stillness in his soul. It was startling to him. He actually enjoyed it. When he was alone in the room, the sound of the clock ticking on the wall was the only thing he could hear. To his surprise, it was rather inviting. Yet, the darkness still lingered, slowly creeping around him like a spider waiting for the proper moment to strike.

Joe took a deep breath. He thought of something C. S. Lewis once said. *The entire universe is moving from beginning to end like a drama.* He marveled at the thought.

Joe closed his eyes and imagined the universe moving to the ticking of the clock, moving him closer and closer to the consummation of all things. *I'll finally be free. No longer will I be trapped. No longer will I experience darkness.*

But that day, he knew, wasn't today. Like a night stalker, the darkness was lurking. Attempting to distract himself, he tried to shift his body in the hospital bed but to no avail. He was too weak. There was nowhere to go. No way to escape the impending doom. His confusion concerning the darkness rocked his understanding of life. He was a Christian. *Why this darkness? Where is the security and peace Jesus promised?*

He was looking forward to seeing Dalia again on Tuesday. He liked her. She was easy to talk to. *Maybe another conversation would get my mind off things? Maybe it would help me forget about the creeping darkness?*

The phrase came rushing back into his mind, and he recited it in his thoughts. *All fears are rooted in the fear of death. How long ago was it when I first heard that homeless man speak those words? Has to be at least fifty years?* It was a blur to him. Yet, as Joe recalled this penetrating phrase yet again, like a tsunami, a mixture of anticipation and dread surfaced in him. He grabbed his handrails again. Joe's soul began to quake, as though he was on the brink of encountering something of a numinous quality. He closed his eyes and took another deep breath.

As Joe steadied himself, he remembered a verse from Psalm 46, *Be still and know that I am God.* The recollection of the verse gave him a small measure of comfort. And while he could not deny the sense of dread, Joe was now also aware of a deeper power sustaining him, a life pulsating inside him. He could tell that he was being prepared for something. Not heaven just yet, that would come in time. No, this was something else. As the conflicting emotions surfaced, Joe did his best to surrender himself to the moment. As he did so, a mist enveloped him.

TWO
HOLY THIRST

The Spirit and the Bride say, "Come." And let the one who hears say, "Come." And let the one who is thirsty come; let the one who desires take the water of life without price.
- Revelation 22:17, ESV

Then, as effortless and illuminating as a sunrise, time shifted, and Joe found himself at his grandmother's kitchen table where he spent much of his childhood. Yet he wasn't a child. Nor was he an eighty-two-year-old on his death bed. He was a young man in good health, perhaps in his thirties. He wasn't quite sure. He was glad to notice that he had clothes on, a light blue button-down short-sleeve shirt that was untucked, and well-worn straight-leg jeans.

His grandmother was there too, yet not as the old woman he remembered her to be. She stood before him a young woman, her short gray hair now replaced with naturally voluminous light brown hair flowing gently over her shoulders. Her simple short-sleeve teal-blue dress, cut to knee length, adorned her young body. Her hazel eyes luminous and clear. Her skin radiant and smooth. Her smile kind. She was beautiful.

"It's so good to see you, Joseph. Please, take a seat. I've prepared some food. Your favorite." She gestured to the seat across from her, his usual place where Joe had sat for home-cooked meals too numerous to count.

"Nonna, is it really you?"

"Yes, Joseph, it's really me." Raising her right hand slightly, she added, "And no, you're not dreaming."

"Then, what is this?" His eyes looked around in wonderment and confusion.

"Well, it's hard to explain. But for your sake, let's call it a vision, somewhere between the present and the future. Something like liminal space, a place of transition."

"I'm aware of all my senses." He looked around. "I can see you . . . and the kitchen." Then, closing his eyes, he took a breath in through his nose. "I can smell the food." He touched his arms, his torso, and his head. "I can feel my body."

"Yes," she said.

"And I can hear you clearly."

"Crazy, isn't it?"

"Will I be able to taste as well?

"Let's find out, shall we?"

The food was simmering in a pot on the small white cooktop adjacent to where he was sitting. She carefully dished out of the large pot what appeared to be homemade cavatelli immersed in a freshly cooked tomato sauce.

She placed the bowl before him along with a large spoon, a napkin, and a healthy glass of red wine that was slightly chilled and then did the same for herself. Then she went to the oven located under the cooktop. From it, she pulled out a warm loaf of freshly cooked bread. She cut it in half with a bread knife and placed both halves on a simple white plate. She then retrieved a small plate of butter along with a small butter knife from the counter behind her.

Joe was mesmerized. *What in the world is going on?* Tentatively, Joe took a spoonful of the pasta. Nonna did the same, following his lead. The sauce was seasoned with fresh garlic that had been peeled and crushed, spread throughout the sauce. Nonna had added just enough salt to bring out the sweetness of the tomatoes. The sauce was also seasoned with a small handful of recently picked basil leaves, which added a slight peppery flavor to the cavatelli. The cavatelli was soft and light, with a smooth texture. He could taste each ingredient complementing the others as he savored them in his mouth. Joe closed his eyes in satisfaction as he swallowed his first bite and then opened them.

"I *can* taste the food!" He nodded in deep satisfaction. He could tell that she was enjoying the moment, watching him eat, just like old times. Nonna took another spoonful from her bowl. Closing her eyes, she chewed and swallowed. Then she let out what seemed to be a satisfying sigh. "Is it as good as you remember Joseph?"

"It's even better. It's absolutely amazing!"

As Joe was finishing that sentence, he caught sight of a candelabra that held three candles: one purple, another red, and the last white, sitting on the far edge of the kitchen countertop near the back door. Each candle was held up by the figure of a person. Each person thrust one hand upward toward the sky, supporting one of the candles overhead, each with one leg extended out toward the center, toes pointed so they touched the toes of the other two figures. The candles were lit. He couldn't be sure, but it looked like they were all in a rhythmic dance.

"The darkness does not define you, Joseph," she said softly.

Joe dropped the spoon as his gut immediately tightened. Fear rose within him, and he took in a sharp breath.

His grandmother sat there quietly as if patiently waiting for Joe to speak again.

But Joe was struggling with what to say.

So, there they sat in a mysterious standoff. The taciturn atmosphere became so unnerving to Joe, more out of frustration than courage, he decided to break the silence. "Should I speak? If so, I'm not sure what I should say."

"How about saying what you want to say instead of searching for what you should say?" she replied with an encouraging tone.

It was a freeing thought to him but also unsettling.

Like a first-year philosophy student attempting to understand the works of Plato, Joe struggled to take in the moment. It now became clear to him that, while the food was outstanding, this encounter was about having a different kind of meal, a verbal exchange that was meant to feed his soul.

"Well, let me start by saying that you look different."

"I guess I should take that as a compliment," she quipped with an engaging smile. He could tell that she was toying with him a little.

"No, I mean you look amazing. You really do."

There was a long, almost deafening silence. Then with a warmth that seemed to flow directly into him, she quietly said, "Thank you."

The tightness in his gut loosened a bit. His eyes welled up with tears as her words disarmed the fear if only for a moment.

"Do you remember the last time I saw you, Nonna?"

"I have some recollection of it, yes. But why don't you refresh my memory."

"You were sitting in your living room, utterly helpless. Your ninety-seven-year-old crippled body was falling apart. Do you remember how confused you were? Do you remember what you said to me?"

"Yes, I think I do," she said softly.

"You said, 'Where's God? Why the darkness? Where has he gone? When will he come for me?'"

She held his gaze as her eyes welled up with tears.

"I had no answer for you, Nonna." There was shame in his voice. "I really wanted to have an answer for you. Some answer that would comfort you. It was the first time a question about God left me speechless."

"But it was more than just a question about God, wasn't it?" she said.

"What do you mean?"

"It was a personal question too. It was *my* question."

He gazed at her while contemplating her words.

"You may not have known it then, but your confusion in that moment marked a very important shift in your life. Yes, it left you speechless . . . and that was good. It quieted all your cliché answers and allowed you to become a better listener to struggling people."

There was a long silence.

"Really? I never would have guessed." He took another spoonful of the cavatelli, relishing it and then swallowing in contentment.

"Not many people notice change the moment it happens. It's imperceptible. It is usually seen best when looking back."

"Oh. Now that you say that, I think it makes a lot of sense," Joe said, mulling over her words.

After a while he said, "Nonna, can I ask you again? What is this time about? Am I getting the message? Am I doing it right? What should I be learning from this?"

"You tend to use that word a lot."

"Which word?"

"Should."

"Oh," he said, thinking about it. "I suppose I do."

"Maybe it would be better to just let things unfold? To worry less about if you're doing things right. To trust that God is somehow in the process?" Her words landed softly and gently. They seemed to highlight something important, something that he was quietly meant to ponder.

"To be honest," she continued, "I'm not entirely sure what this time is about myself. All I know is that our time together is meant to get you a little further down the road."

He cocked his head to the side. "Which road is that?"

She thought about it for a moment and then said, "The salvation road."

"Huh," he awkwardly replied, while his mind worked to process her words. Attempting to relax a little more, Joe took a sip of the red wine and relished its cool smoothness as he swallowed.

He broke off a piece of the bread and spread a generous portion of butter on it. He took a bite. The outside of the bread was crispy; he could hear the crackle of the crust as he began to chew. The inside was warm and soft. The butter was creamy with a hint of saltiness that had permeated every crevice of the soft interior.

"Nonna, can you be more specific? What do you mean by the salvation road?"

"It's the process of salvation. We come to know God by opening our souls to his Son, Jesus. This is where salvation begins but not where it ends. There is so much more. You've been on the salvation road for a long, long time. God has been forming and shaping you along the way, starting when you came to know him and then faithfully, patiently, even delightfully, continuing his work in you for all these years."

"I believe you, but frankly it's been hard to see for myself. Most of the time I have been aware of my relational failures, and the awareness of my failures only seemed to grow as I have gotten older. I know God loves me. God knows I have told countless people about his love for them. But if I am to be honest, I've had so much trouble receiving his love for myself. Don't get me wrong, I trust that his love is real. The cross leaves no doubt in my mind. Well, except when the darkness comes and I wonder if there's a God at all. It's just in personal experience, well, that's where I have struggled."

"Believe it or not, your struggle with seeing more of your sin is not necessarily bad. The closer one draws near to God, the more one becomes aware of all that still gets in the way. What does the Bible say? 'Walk in the light as he is in the light, and the blood of his Son, Jesus, cleanses you from all sin.' If you are going to walk in his light, you are going to see more of your sin, more of your relational failure. It's actually a sign of maturity."

Joe placed his forearms on the edge of the table, supporting his upper torso while his hands moved to the rhythm of his words. He broke off another piece of bread. "So if what you're saying is true, then spiritual maturity is counterintuitive?" he mused.

"Yes!" She clasped her palms together in front of her. "That's why some have called it the upside down kingdom of God. Yet, in reality, God is the one who is right side up. *We* are actually upside down. It only feels opposite because God is moving one way"—she threw one hand wide to the right as if waving a flag—"and the entire human race is moving the other way." She threw her other hand wide to the left with the same motion. "One of your sages once said, 'To everyone who is running off a cliff, the one who is running the other way seems crazy.'" She spoke these words with passion.

Like fireflies in early summer, these thoughts lingered in Joe's mind. He looked over at the candelabra. Such a beautiful picture of three persons dancing together. It made him wonder about the reality of things. A deep yearning to know God better began to stir his inner being. He thought about the Trinity, dancing in rhythmic motion. He longed to be caught up in their community of love. Joe's demeanor had shifted as he gazed at the candles, and he was aware that Nonna could tell.

"What's going on in you as you look at the candles?"

He was immediately drawn to the question. It touched on something deep within him. "I am aware of an intense longing to know God better, to be caught up in God, to be with God. I want to know the Father better. I want to know Jesus better. I want to know the Holy Spirit better. More than that, I long to be with them. Forever."

"Ah, you're in touch with your holy thirst," she said as she leaned forward, placing the palm of her right hand close to him, almost touching his chest.

"Yes, although I have never called it 'holy thirst.' Yet, hearing it now, that phrase seems to describe my deep longing very well. Yes, I think I like that phrase, 'holy thirst.' But . . ."

"But?" she replied.

"But if I'm honest. It hasn't always been easy living with my holy thirst."

"Would you like to say more?" she said with a look of anticipation on her face.

Joe was aware of her desire to draw his soul out into the open, and he appreciated the opportunity to put words to his struggle.

"Well, a thirst implies the lack of something. It implies living with something that is coming later, something I want now but don't have right now." He hesitated for a moment and then said, "That's not a comfortable feeling. There is part of me that would rather feel full and satisfied right now. To make it worse, the culture over the years seemed to reinforce the message of satisfaction now, even church culture."

"You've been learning something different?"

"I think so . . . yet."

"Yet what?"

"It gets confusing because Jesus told the woman at the well that if she drank the water he had to give, she would never be thirsty again."

"Yes, I can see why that could be confusing."

"Do you have any thoughts on that, Nonna?"

"I think so." She leaned a bit forward, placing her elbows on the table and her forefinger on her chin. "Remember, Joseph, the woman at the well was coming to know Jesus for the first time. He was introducing himself to her. She had not rightly identified her holy thirst and was trying to fill it illegitimately."

"Through relationships with different men that never seemed to work."

"Yes," she said, now pointing her forefinger in the air. "In a certain sense his words were true. Once she came to know Jesus, she never thirsted again as she once did. Or to put it a different way, she was never again *enslaved* to lesser thirsts. That was important for her to know in the moment. He could have said much more. But he stopped there, for her sake."

Joe pondered her words. He could tell that she was waiting to continue until he had digested what she had already said. Joe responded, "I think I'm with you so far."

Nonna continued, "Now, think about Jesus's final invitation to *Christians* in the book of Revelation. Do you remember what Jesus said?"

"Let all those who are thirsty come."

"Yes again." She shook her forefinger in the air. "It was an invitation for all Christians to stay thirsty for him."

"How paradoxical! How countercultural!"

"It is, Joseph. One of your sages once said, 'O God, the triune God, I want to want thee; I long to be filled with longing; I thirst to be made more thirsty still.' I think he was getting the hang of it."

He leaned forward a bit. "I really like that, Nonna. Yes. I think you're right," Joe mused. "He seemed to be onto something important." Joe took a sip of wine and then asked another question. "Nonna, would you say that when we embrace our holy thirst, instead of trying to fill it, we live better, love better?"

She gave it some thought. "What would you say, Joseph?"

"I knew you were going to ask me that question." They laughed again.

Sitting back in his chair, he thought for a moment. "I would say yes. When I was a young Christian, I thought it was perfectly legitimate to fill my thirst with accolades from other people. You could say that I was addicted to accolades. Some people are drug addicts. I was trying to fill my holy thirst with recognition. In fact, I remember a certain night when I lectured on C. S. Lewis at Bristol Hall. I was in the zone, so to speak, and people were really tracking with me. Several of my students came up to me afterward, congratulating me, probing me for more insights. I was over the moon. Yet, when Maria and I were driving home after the lecture, I came down from my recognition high. All the good words given to me were not enough. They all leaked out like water from a broken well. When I asked her what she thought about the night, she turned to me with a weary smile. 'It was good, honey. Can we leave it alone though? I've got a lot on my mind.' That was the first time I became aware how my need for recognition weighed on her. As I confessed that to God, I began to love her a bit better. I became more curious about her and less needy about me. Come to find out that the night of that lecture, Maria was worried about relational tensions taking place with our son, Patrick. It led to a good conversation. Living with holy thirst is tough, but it yields the fruit of the Spirit. At least that's what I've been learning over the years."

"What a wonderful story!" She clapped her hands slightly as she said those words. "Something good transpired in you that night. You deeply ministered to Maria. True ministry has to do with loving people, not running programs. You became more concerned with your wife and less concerned about the success of your class. Yes, you moved rather well with Maria. Not perfectly of course, but nevertheless, your curiosity touched a deep place in her. The Lord was well pleased with you. There is good going on inside of you, more than you realize. The darkness doesn't define you, Joseph. The life of God defines you." Instinctively they both looked at the candelabra.

Her words were a soothing balm applied to a raw soul, and Joe wanted to bask in them. An affection rose within him. To see her looking so vibrant and hearing her kind, perceptive words was more than he could contain. He reached his hands over the table to grasp hers. Stumbling over his words, Joe searched for some way of expressing his affection for her. "Oh, Nonna, I love . . . what I mean to say is that I so appreciate . . ." Yet, the moment their hands touched, everything went pitch dark.

THREE
A QUESTION OF ETERNITY

*If we find ourselves with a desire that nothing in this world
can satisfy, the most probable explanation is that
we were made for another world.*
- *C. S. Lewis,* The Weight of Glory

Joe suddenly awoke in his hospital bed with what he only could imagine was a panic attack. Or was it a heart attack? The symptoms were so similar it was hard to tell. His breathing was labored, and he seemed to be gasping for air. His palms were sweating. There was pain in his left arm, which crawled into his chest.

"Is it my time? Lord, into your hands I commit my spirit." Joe said these words with a quivering voice. He wanted his last words on earth to be spiritual. Or did he want them to at least sound spiritual? He wasn't sure. *Could spiritual posturing be present within me even on my death bed?*

It boggled his mind to think that the energy of sin could be influencing his last words on earth. Yet, strangely enough, it freed Joe to ponder the immense grace of his God. As this thought ruminated in his mind, the thirst inside him to see the human face of God, to see Jesus, deepened even more.

So, Joe was more than a bit disappointed when the panic attack subsided and his breathing calmed. He was still around after all. Yes, the lingering of the dying process proved difficult. However, it was the prolonging of his longing for God that proved most difficult.

Days went by until it was Tuesday. His mind consumed with thoughts of heaven. He remembered Nonna's holy impatience while she was dying. Now, he was in that same place. *Lord, why do you still have me here?* The moment he finished saying those words, Dalia walked through the door.

"Oh, you're awake. It's nice to see you again, Joe." She gently knelt beside him. "How are you doing today?"

"Well, I'm still here."

"You don't sound all that excited about that fact."

"You're perceptive, Dalia." They couldn't help but chuckle a little.

Joe could tell by the inquisitive look in her eyes that she wanted to ask something.

"Do you have a question for me?"

"Actually, I do."

"Go ahead, Dalia. You can ask."

"Well, I really don't want to intrude."

"It's only intrusive if I don't want you to ask. Please, go ahead."

"Okay." She tensely grasped her hands together in her lap and proceeded. "You're really looking forward to dying?

You really believe that there is something after this life? Something good waiting for you?"

"Yes, I really do."

"Huh," she said as she looked down.

Joe gently said, "You don't think so?"

"I'm not quite sure myself. There was a time when the thought of an afterlife piqued my curiosity, but not so much anymore."

There was a long, awkward pause. Joe wondered if she was speaking out of a wound. He proceeded with some caution. "Dalia, answer this only if you want to: Did something happen that caused you to stop being curious?"

She stood up and shook off the question as though it was a stiff breeze.

"Look at you, Joe. You're not scheduled for a shower today, but how about we get you into some clean clothes. I bet you would feel better. How about it?"

Sensing her obvious reluctance to continue, he said, "That would be great. Let's do it. Thanks."

She walked over to the tall dresser near the picture of Maria and pulled out a pair of sweatpants, a tee shirt, a loose-fitting flannel shirt, a clean pair of calf-high socks. Putting on some nitrile gloves, she very gently took off his shirt, unbuttoning the front, removing his arms one sleeve at a time, making sure to move slowly enough so as not to cause any pain. She occasionally watched his face for any signs of grimacing.

Joe reassured her. "You're doing great, Dalia." She smiled at him.

The dirty tee shirt was a bit more difficult, but she managed to get him out of it, bending each arm very slowly, pulling out the shirt so his elbow went through first and then forearm and hand, then finally gently lifting it off his head. Then she took a warm cloth and wiped down his chest, arms, and neck.

It soothed Joe. "Ah, thank you, Dalia."

Taking her time, she then put the new tee shirt on using the same technique only this time backwards, and the flannel shirt over the tee shirt, to keep him warm. Changing his long pants was a little easier. They were loose enough for her to gently pull them off, both pant legs simultaneously. Before putting his clean sweats on, she checked his brief. It was wet. "Do you mind if I change you, Joe?" she asked.

"If *you* don't mind. Sure."

She unfastened the tabs, gently rolled him on his side and then removed his wet brief. Taking another warm cloth, she gently cleansed his front side and back side, then put the new brief into place and rolled him onto his back. She fastened the new brief so it was snug but not too tight.

Dalia exchanged her soiled nitrile gloves for a new pair. She put his clean sweats on with relative ease. She took his socks off, one at a time. With another warm cloth, she washed his feet.

Joe couldn't help but think of Jesus washing the disciples' feet. He marveled at how gently she changed him. "That was a gift. Thank you so much."

She smiled at him again. Then she gingerly put on each sock and placed his blanket on him so it covered his body from feet to shoulders.

"Would you like your head propped up a bit?"

"Yes, I would appreciate that very much."

She grabbed the controller for the hospital bed and propped Joe's head up so that he was in a comfortable position. After which, Dalia sat in her chair awkwardly, rubbing the top of her thighs.

Taking a bit of a risk, Joe said, "Earlier you asked me if I believed in an afterlife. I told you that I do. However, there is much more to the story. I wonder, would you like to hear about my spiritual journey? I would love to share some of it with you if you have the time? If you don't want to hear or if you don't have the time, I understand. Just thought I would ask."

To his surprise, she said, "Well, yes, I would love to hear part of your spiritual story. I have a little time before my next appointment. Would you like to share some now?"

"Yes. I'd love to."

She leaned forward in her chair, looking somewhat tense.

He smiled at her. "Why don't you lean back in your chair and take a breath. Let my story just wash over you. Just be aware of what might resonate with you. Also, be aware of what raises questions as well. You don't need to try to absorb it all."

She smiled broadly. "I think I needed to hear that. Thank you." She leaned back and took a breath.

"Where to start. Yes. OK. Well, I grew up in an Italian American home. It was a fairly good life. We lived in a good neighborhood. My parents made a decent living. All my material needs were provided for. We went to church occasionally, but there was nothing compelling about the church I attended. It seemed to produce more guilt in me than freedom. The messages all had the same three themes. For instance: 'God says be kind to people. You're not being kind enough. Try harder.' Or 'God says pray more. You're not praying enough. Try harder.' Or 'God says read your

Bible more. You're not reading enough. Try harder.' And on it went. All that did was deepen my sense of guilt. I could never live up to the message. But I went because it was expected. I got used to tuning out the message. As I grew older, I found more familiarity among people who did not believe in God. The idea that I could captain my own soul, live my own life autonomously, was very compelling. I couldn't do it God's way, so why not try to do it my way? I decided I was an atheist. I stopped believing in a God altogether.

"Nevertheless, I liked thinking about the meaning of life, which drew me to study philosophy in college. Later, I got a PhD in philosophy, so I could teach. I excelled at my craft and became an excellent debater. I could run circles around others who challenged me about the meaning of life. At times I used to debate Christians. Even though they disagreed with me, they were respectful, a quality I despised and considered weak.

"Once, I debated a Christian in front of a group of my colleagues. My arguments were lucid and persuasive. He had no idea how to respond. The problem, which I did not see at the time, was that I was also exceedingly cruel. I not only put my opponent in his place, I humiliated him. He never challenged me again. In fact, he never spoke to me again, which I could not understand. In reality, I was clueless and conceited. It turned out that captaining my own soul was destroying my relationships, not to mention the damage to my own soul. I had no clue."

Dalia placed her elbow on the arm of her chair and rested her head in her hand.

Joe could tell he had her attention. "During family gatherings, I would often spout about my latest philosophical discoveries. I liked to talk about myself. There was no room for curiosity about others. Those who were closest to me felt the pain of my self-obsession. But after many years of striving to be the center of my own life, I came to realize that it just wasn't working. The self-promotion was suffocating my soul, drowning out the voices of my friends and family. None of them wanted to be around me. Looking back, I couldn't blame them. Everything was about me. I cared for no one. I had no capacity to give, no capacity to love. Then it all came crashing down around me Christmas Eve, 1965.

"I was living in Seattle, single at the time. That particular night, it was pouring down rain. I sat on my covered porch, alone and in anguish. No one, not even my family members, invited me for the holidays. They all had convenient excuses. It was the first time I felt utterly alone.

"I went inside and turned on the TV, searching for a mindless show. There was a teacher speaking to a small congregation somewhere. I despised televangelists. But this guy . . . he was different. He didn't yell. He didn't use fancy spiritual words. He wasn't preaching the 'try harder' message. He just talked . . . and I was strangely drawn to his words."

Joe tried to lift himself higher in the bed using the handrails.

"Wait, let me help you, Joe," she replied. Dalia walked to the head of his bed, put her hands under his armpits, and gently pulled him up.

"Is that better?"

"Yes, that's much better. Thanks. Now, where was I?"

"The teacher," Dalia said as she returned to her seat.

"Oh yes, the teacher. He talked about how we were not designed to captain our own souls, calling it a foolish direction that would only lead to isolation. It piqued my interest. He talked about how all humans have masks they wear, which keep our real selves from being known. Those words struck me to the core. Was I wearing the mask of competence? Did I live for the respect of others? Yet, even if it were true, I saw no way out, no way to truly change."

Dalia was still listening, but it was difficult for Joe to read her response. She appeared motionless, her eyes looking up slightly, with neither a smile nor a frown.

Joe pressed on anyway. "He went on to say that Jesus was the only one that could change the direction of a person's life. Jesus was able to change people from the inside out. His death on the cross, taking the penalty for our sins, rising on the third day, defeating sin and death once and for all, had made true change possible. He quoted a verse from the New Testament, 'Behold, I stand at the door and knock. If anyone hears my voice and opens the door, I will come in to him and eat with him, and he with me.' Change from the inside out, Dalia. That's what really struck me. All my fragile arguments, like a house of cards, came crashing down. I received Jesus Christ as my Savior that very night. Life was never the same. I began to slowly change, like the teacher said, from the inside out."

After Joe finished speaking, they sat in silence for a while. Dalia was still sitting back in her chair with her hands together and fingers interlocked resting on her lap. She was looking up toward the ceiling with her eyes closed.

"A penny for your thoughts?" Joe finally said.

"Well, I'm not even sure what I'm thinking at the moment."

"Oh. Well, that's okay. Maybe you just need time to ponder it."

"Perhaps," she replied.

Joe sensed the tension between them. He was sure Dalia sensed it too. The silence was thick enough to cut with a knife.

Adjusting herself in her seat, Dalia said, "Actually, I have a question. But . . ." She hesitated.

"Go ahead," Joe said.

She looked around. "Before I continue, can I get you something to drink? You've been talking for a while. You must be a bit parched."

"Now that you mention it, yes, I am thirsty. There should be some bottled water in the small refrigerator near the nurses' station. Would you mind getting me one?"

"Not at all. I'd be glad to get you one." She got up and started to leave the room.

"Oh and please feel free to get one for yourself."

"Thanks."

While Dalia was grabbing the water, Joe happened to glance out of the big bay window on the other side of the room. Just outside his window, hanging like a chandelier from the branch of an oak tree, was the lit candelabra. The colors were the same, deep purple, crimson red, the pure white of a dove. It was identical in appearance to the one he saw in Nonna's kitchen. He gazed at the candelabra, entranced. His holy thirst ignited, he thought of the Father, Son, and Holy Spirit and what it must be like to be with them in heaven. He longed all the more for the day he would cross the threshold, when he would see Jesus face to face. He looked away from the candelabra and blinked several times. When he looked back, the candelabra was gone.

When Dalia returned, Joe was peering upward as if through the ceiling.

"What's going on?"

"Oh, well, just thinking about something."

"Something important."

"Yes, something very important."

"You want to talk about it?"

"At some point, absolutely. But I would rather hear your question, Dalia."

"Okay. Whatever you think best." She opened both bottles of water and put a straw in Joe's. It was a bit too heavy for Joe to hold so she brought it up to his lips. Joe took a few long satisfying sips.

"You said something about being changed from the inside out. Can you elaborate on that a bit?" said Dalia.

"I think I can. May I first inquire as to why you're asking the question?"

"Yeah, I asked the question because most people look at me and see a competent and caring person. They're not entirely wrong. I think I'm good at what I do, and I enjoy doing it."

"It shows!" Joe said, wanting to confirm her words.

"The thing is . . . I don't feel that way on the inside. There are things that haunt me, conflicting emotions, that I find hard to put into words. No one would guess I was such a mess on the inside. I put up a pretty good front. Yet, when you mentioned Jesus wanting to change us from the inside out, it made me wonder if he was the sort of person that really wanted to know what was going on inside of people."

"He absolutely is that kind of person. Great deduction! In fact, there is a Bible verse that speaks about this directly. Can I share it with you?"

"I'd love to hear it."

"This is from the Old Testament. These are God's words

to one of his prophets. It comes from First Samuel chapter 16 verse 7. It says, 'People look at the outward appearance, but the Lord looks at the heart.'"

"Huh," she said. "It really says that?"

"Yes. It certainly does. When I was listening to that teacher in Seattle, I kept hearing his invitation to drop the mask, to acknowledge who I was on the inside, a complete mess. In fact, it's the only way to truly come to God, as we truly are on the inside, not what we pretend to be on the outside."

"Oh," she said, nervously rubbing her hands together.

It was apparent to Joe that she had more emotional cards to play. He was more convinced now that there was a wound inside of her that she kept under lock and key. He wondered what it might be.

Looking at her watch, she said, "Oh my goodness look at the time! I really need to be going. Got to get to my next appointment. Joe, thanks for sharing part of your story. I really appreciate it. You've given me a lot to chew on. Now, can I get you anything else before I go?"

He wanted to ask more questions, to hear more from her, but also wanted to respect her time. "No, I'm good. Maybe we could talk more about it next time I see you?"

"I'll definitely think about it. Today is Tuesday. I'll be back on Thursday to give you a shower. Time permitting, maybe we can talk then?"

"Sounds good."

"So, I'll see you then, Joe?"

"See you then, Dalia."

With that, she gathered her things and slipped out the door.

After she left, Joe lay in his hospital bed with his head

slightly propped up, thinking about their conversation. He thought over what they discussed, Dalia's curiosity about the afterlife, Joe's opportunity to share his spiritual journey, her perception about Jesus being someone who seeks after authentic hearts. Then there was the possible wound in Dalia. Joe could not help but think how her wound, up to this point in her life, had squelched her curiosity about the afterlife. Yet, it was clear things were changing. She was beginning to ask questions. *Is the door of her heart beginning to open?* He longed for Dalia to be set free, for her to come to know Jesus. She was becoming more than his hospice CNA. She was becoming a friend.

His mind went to the image of the candelabra. *What was that about?* He thought of the Father, Son, and Spirit moving in a rhythmic circle, enjoying each other's company. He yearned to be present with them in their mutual enjoyment of each other. He longed to enjoy them, and to be enjoyed by them, forever.

Yet the darkness was still prowling, triggering fears that were unreasonable but nevertheless very real. Irrational questions came flooding back into his mind. *What good is my life? What possible purpose could there be as I lie in this hospital bed, taking up space? Where are you, God? What do you want from me? Haven't I walked the salvation road long enough? When will you come for me? How long will you be silent? Are you real?* His fists were clenched. His gut swirled with fear. Joe was so unnerved by the silence his whole body began to shake. *God, why don't you cut me a break!* No response. Just the ticking of the clock on the far wall.

He thought of the story of Job, one of the oldest stories in the Old Testament. He recalled Job's spiritual breakdown and eventual recovery. He was drawn to the man's anger, his anguish, even his accusations. *Dang, what I would do just to have a cup of coffee with that guy!*

Unexpectedly, like a spinning top, the room began to spin, faster and faster until Joe's hospital bed began to give way to centrifugal force. His bed slammed against the open bay window, catapulting Joe through it into the open air. Joe was caught off guard and disoriented as he aimlessly rotated through the sky. He was spinning so fast he found it hard to focus. He grasped at the air, hoping to take hold of something that might break his fall. At the mercy of gravity, he closed his eyes and braced for impact . . . but it never came.

When Joe opened his eyes, he was a young thirty-something again, sitting at a table in one of his favorite coffee shops. It was a quaint place, ten wooden tables each having at least two wooden chairs. They were arranged in a close circle situated around a fireplace with a large flagstone hearth on all four sides. Joe was seated so close to the fireplace he could reach out and touch it with is hand. The warmth from the fireplace shrouded Joe like a cozy blanket. Small flames were enveloping the wood in the fireplace, but strangely the wood did not appear to be burning. There was a long table made out of a beautiful dark granite slab with silver veins running through it against the wall in the back of the coffee shop. It had all manner of pastries strewn about: blueberry scones, chocolate almond croissants, lemon pound cake, ricotta-filled cannolis, cinnamon muffins, fudge brownies, and many more. A rich fragrance of coffee hung in the air. He noticed two large mugs filled with a fresh brew at the table, a cup of whole cream, and a bowl of sugar with a little spoon.

There, sitting opposite from him was a man. Joe looked

around and surmised that they were the only two in the place. The man was young in appearance, wearing a white tunic with a golden sash around his waist. He had short brown hair and a thick beard with one very slight streak of gray. By the look of his physique, he had well-defined muscles. While the man looked calm, he also had a wildness to his appearance.

Joe's initial reaction was one of ambivalence. *Who is this guy? Can he be trusted?* He was still attempting to regain his equilibrium from the strange way he entered into this bizarre scene. He finally got a handle on his composure long enough to size up this man again. His eyes had a piercing look while his smile seemed genuinely inviting. They both sat there quietly.

Finally, the man spoke as the edges of his mouth turned slightly upward. "Be careful what you ask for, Joseph."

Wait a minute. It couldn't be.

"Yes, it's me, Joseph."

The man sitting opposite Joseph Tropea was the man himself. It was Job.

FOUR
THE RADICAL PRESENT

God loves you unconditionally, as you are and not as you
should be, because nobody is as they should be.
- Brennan Manning, All Is Grace

Joe was silent more out of shock than anything else, his mouth slightly agape.

He waited for Job to say something, but he sat there quietly. Joe tried to say something, but every time he opened his mouth, no words came out. He was finding it difficult to come to terms with the fact that he was sitting with Job, whose tragic story was one of the oldest in the Bible. Job had lost all his wealth. Then his ten children died. After which, he broke out with boils. This led to his wife's nervous breakdown. On top of it all, he lost his stellar reputation. All of which happened in one day.

I have no idea what to say to this guy.

So, there they sat. The silence between them produced a

tension that made Joe squirm in his chair. "Should I be the one to speak?" Joe said nervously.

"I hear you have a fondness for that word."

"Which word?"

"Should."

Joe closed his eyes tight, sighing deeply.

"There I go again." He shook his head.

Job leaned forward in his chair and smiled. "You're in good company, Joseph."

"Ugh. Well, that's kind of you to say."

"It's the truth. We all must learn that living in freedom takes more courage than living by scripts or formulas. Better to speak what we feel and not what we ought to say."

Joe took those words in, wondering if he, just then, had inched down the salvation road.

They lingered in silence for a while.

"She's quite an amazing woman."

"Huh?" Joe was thrown off balance.

"Your grandmother."

"Oh, yes . . . so you have met her?"

"Yes, I have. She has so much affection for you."

Joe's heart warmed at those words. "Thanks for saying that. I have a lot of affection for her."

There was another slight pause in the conversation.

"I get the impression that you're a very wise man," Joe said.

"Yes, I am. Yet, it wasn't always that way. As you know from my earthly story, I spoke a lot. Much of the time my words were foolish."

"Yes, I recall. Oh, well, I mean. I recall from your story. Not that I judged you or want to judge you now . . ." Joe was doing his best to backpedal. After a long uncomfortable silence, embarrassed by his words, he said, "I didn't mean to offend you."

Job replied, "No offense taken. You have spoken well." He said these words with such tenderness, with such a non-defensive spirit, it made Joe wonder about the nature of true living, the kind of living where a person never worried about the opinions of others but could speak the truth with such ease, even if the words highlighted something deeply wrong about themselves.

"Now that I think about it, you also seem to be a man at rest," Joe said.

"You have spoken well again. Although it has taken a long while to get to the place where I am today. One could say that I not only stumbled down the salvation road but at times fought the journey tooth and nail."

With that statement, Joe knew he was in good company. *Now I remember why I wanted to have coffee with him.* He took a moment to stir cream and sugar into his coffee, while Job followed suit. They lifted their cups and clinked them together before they both took a sip.

"Let's go get some pastries, shall we?" Job said with excitement in his voice.

"Sure! They look fantastic."

They got up and walked over to the desserts. Joe couldn't decide between the ricotta-filled cannoli or the lemon pound cake. So he took both. Job smiled at him and grabbed a fudge brownie. Then they walked back to their table and eased back into their chairs.

Joe picked up the cannoli. The outside softly crumbled as he took a bite while the sweet creamy filling melted in his mouth. After swallowing, Joe said, "I have some questions for you."

"Fantastic. Start with the one that seems most alive in you," said Job as he took a bite of his fudge brownie, closing his eyes in what appeared to be deep satisfaction.

"What's most alive in me? I like that. OK." Joe had to think a bit.

Before Joe could speak, Job added while licking his fingers, "Take your time. We are not in any kind of hurry. Neither is God."

Joe took a deep breath in, exhaled, and relaxed into his chair. "Why does it all have to be so difficult?" He blurted out the words.

Job remained silent for a long period of time. His voice became even more steady, more at ease. "Be more specific," he said with seemingly no hint of irritation.

"Life."

"What about life?"

Appreciating the curiosity, Joe continued. "I look back on my life, and while there is deep gratitude, there is also a lot of disappointment. I thought I would have been further along by now. I thought I would be more, you know, godly. I didn't expect to struggle so much."

"Which begs the question," Job replied, "what is the nature of true godliness?"

Joe jumped in. "Many churches in my day would have answered that question with one word, obedience. I was never drawn to it. I'm not saying obedience is wrong. It just seems that there needs to be more than sheer, willful, grit-your-teeth obedience. Otherwise, something important gets missed. That's how I see it if I am to be honest."

"Ah yes. Obedience," replied Job. "I gave that one a go for a long time. I was under the assumption that if I remained obedient to God then everything else in my life would fall into place. I had my life wired like a finely tuned piano. If that wasn't enough, I even offered sacrifices to God for the sake of my kids, just in case one of them had done something wrong. It seemed to work for a very long time. Yes, obedience. That tune will play for many Christians who are seeking a formula for living. Yet, here's the thing: We can be obedient to God's laws while our hearts are far from him. It's a very seductive tune. One that sounds more like a dirge than a dance to God's ears."

Joe intuitively knew this was true, yet it was good to hear someone put words to his gut instinct. "Just hearing you say that makes me feel less crazy. You have my attention."

"As you have mine, Joseph. Your anger is to some degree very justified. God has something much more beautiful in mind than just making us obedient. He wants to change our hearts from the inside out, and that requires a deep transformation. Part of that transformation has to do with seeing God for who he really is."

Almost imperceptibly, Joe's eyes refocused like the lens of a camera changing from telescopic to a wide angle. That was when he caught sight of it. It was the lit candelabra that he saw in Nonna's kitchen and on the tree outside his bay window. It was now sitting on the adjacent table near one of the windows of the coffee shop. The vibrant colors of royal purple, crimson red, and the pure white of a dove, came together to stir up a kaleidoscope of hope that was again surfacing in Joe's heart. His holy thirst was now ignited like the embers of a glowing fire. He gazed at the candles as if transfixed. His mind was now meandering and wondering again about the deepest nature of reality. He could not tear his gaze away from this beautiful image. Nor did he want to. Joe remained mesmerized for a long while.

He also noticed something different. This candelabra was slowly rotating.

He finally looked back at Job with surprise, wondering if he too had seen the rotating candles. He was looking at Joe with tears welling up in his eyes. By the kind look on his face, they seemed to be tears of joy.

"Take your time, Joseph. Like I said, we're in no hurry here. Neither is God."

It was worth hearing it a second time, especially to Joe whose hurry-up-and-change-me attitude toward God was legendary, especially to those who knew him well.

Joe gathered himself and found the strength to form another question. "So, how did you make the change from mere obedience to deep transformation?"

"I didn't make the change, Joseph. When it comes to change, God is always in charge. Yes, we do have a part to play in our own transformation, but it's a minor part compared to the Father, Son, and Holy Spirit."

At the sound of their threefold name, a slight quake of happiness rumbled like thunder in his depths, if for but a moment sounding off a prophetic call of what lay ahead of Joe when he finally crossed the threshold into heaven.

"Fair enough. So how did God make the change?"

"A much better question. Let me start by saying it took time."

"I'm beginning to hear a theme."

"I'm glad." They exchanged a knowing chuckle. Joe leaned forward and took a bite of the lemon pound cake. It was rich and moist with a zesty lemon flavor followed by a dense crumb that easily fell apart in his mouth.

Then, Job's face grew serious but not in a way that

extinguished even a minutia of joy. "The anguish was the first thing that surfaced. As you know, my three friends had come to see me. They started off really well, sitting with me in the silence for seven days. Sometimes, that's all suffering people need, friends who are willing to sit with them in the silence. They would have done well if they had stopped there. But as you know, they didn't." He paused with a look of inquiry on his face to see if Joe had a response. It appeared to be a gentle gesture to make sure that Joe was still following the flow of the conversation.

"I'm following," Joe said, interpreting Job's silence correctly.

Job nodded approvingly with a warm smile. "I cursed the day of my birth. I cursed God for bringing me into existence. I raised my internal fist toward heaven and demanded a reply from God, fully assured in my own heart that, like a misjudged defendant in a courtroom, I would be proven innocent."

While Joe recalled this from his own reading of the book of Job, to hear the words from Job himself brought deep understanding to his struggle, again replacing craziness with sanity.

"As you already know, Joseph, this anger-filled response was more than a bit surprising for my friends. To be frank, they were unnerved by it. They were expecting me to handle things with more spiritual composure, with more spiritual balance. Yet, knowing Jesus has really *nothing* to do with balance. Jesus was working deeply in my situation although I did not know him by name yet. In fact it was all three, the Father, the Son, and the Holy Spirit working together to accomplish a much deeper work within me. My friends wanted me to manage my anguish, even to suppress it. God, however, wanted to surface it."

"Wow, did you just say that out loud?" quipped Joe.

As they laughed together, it became more clear to Joe that both of them were enjoying this newfound comradery. Yet, Joe could see that all of this was more for his own benefit. While Job seemed to be enjoying the growing friendship, he also seemed complete in a way Joe had yet to fully understand. Job seemed to be enjoying the passion that emerged from giving what he had for the benefit of another. There was nothing at stake for him anymore. His delight in giving seemed as natural as Babe Ruth hitting a fastball out of the park.

"That seems like a very important distinction. Can you say more about that? Why would God want to surface your anguish?"

"I had just lost my seven sons and three daughters, my physical health taken from me. My wife was having a nervous breakdown. Those who used to admire me for how well my life was going suddenly began to avoid me. Anguish was the most immediate response of my shredded soul. God wanted to meet me where I truly was, not where I pretended to be. In fact, that is the only way to encounter God, in the place where we truly are, in the radical present."

"The radical present?"

"Where we are in this very moment, not the next moment, not the previous moment, but right now, in this present moment. He is always in the radical present, waiting for us."

A silence enveloped them.

Job finally said, "Make sense?"

"More than you could possibly know," Joe said with a gratifying sigh.

Job continued, "In all honesty, I had no clue what God was up to while I was suffering. But much later on I realized it was something incredibly good. He wanted me to stop playing games with him. He wanted me to be exactly where I was. He also wanted me to see what was beneath the anguish."

Joe took a moment to take a sip of his coffee, thinking about what Job just said.

"Beneath the anguish, you say?"

"Yes, beneath the anguish. I could not see what was beneath the anguish if I never owned the anguish as my own."

A rhythmic pause, like a fermata lengthening the note of a song, entered into the conversation. Joe didn't know whether to speak or to wait for this symphony of words to continue. "Thanks so much for what you just said. It means a lot. It helps me remember what a paradox this salvation road presents. As you can probably guess, I'm wondering what was underneath your anguish. Something important, I would suspect."

"An entitled spirit." Job did not hesitate in his answer.

"A what?" replied Joe, reeling from what felt like a cold bucket of water thrown in his face.

Job remained silent, allowing the words to sink in a bit more.

"I don't understand," Joe said. But deep down he did, at least a little bit.

"An entitled spirit. An internal fist in God's face."

"Oh. Huh. Well. I see. I think."

"None of us see it all that well. We tend to see it more in others than in ourselves. Having said that, I believe you, Joseph. I know you are trying to grapple with what I am saying to you, and that's better than just accepting something because someone else says it."

Joe let out a sigh of relief and simply said, "Thank you." The tenderness in their relationship seemed to ripen with that exchange of words. These were weighty things Joe was pondering, but they could not have been received well if Joe had not heard the affection pouring forth from the voice of this great giant of the faith.

"So let me see if I understand. God allowed tremendous suffering to come into your life and then remained silent in order to surface what was most immediately in you, your anguish. The reason why he wanted to surface your anguish was to offer you freedom to be where you really were and not where you pretended to be. He wanted you to stop playing spiritual games with him. He wanted to take the pressure off you, the pressure that comes from trying to please him so that you can have what you want, a blessed life with no suffering. He wanted more than blind obedience. He wanted your heart."

"You're doing well so far."

"But God wasn't finished. He wanted to surface something else. Something deeper in you than the anguish. A bigger problem. He wanted to surface your entitled spirit, the internal fist inside of you, the fist you were shaking in God's face."

"You've spoken well, Joseph."

"Really? I'm not sure I even know what I'm talking about."

"It doesn't matter that you don't entirely understand.

Just do your best to stay in the flow of the conversation and keep following the rhythm of the Holy Spirit."

As Joe heard those words, his gaze immediately went to the rotating candelabra. The Spirit shared between the Father and the Son was the Holy Spirit, the white dove. *So I can follow the Holy Spirit's rhythm? What does that actually mean?*

Job did nothing to disturb the pondering that was happening in Joe. The silence that Job provided by staying quiet created a sacred space in which Joe could linger, giving the Holy Spirit elbow room to move within him as he so desired. Joe finally snapped out of his meditative state like someone waking suddenly from a vivid dream.

"Oh, sorry, I was lost in thought. Can you say more about the entitled spirit? I will be honest with you. There is part of me that wants to resist what you are saying and another part of me that resonates with it. So much of the time, I have heard of sin being described as behavioral sin, things we do that are wrong. But you seem to be saying something more. You're not talking about the things we do wrong. You seem to be talking about the way we relate, an energy embedded deep inside of us that is stubborn to all reason, not something we can actually change by modifying our behavior. Am I even close?"

"You are close. Well spoken, Joseph. By outward appearance, I was leading a pretty good life. Most people were impressed by all of my sacrifices, my noble prayers, my good-looking family, my wealth and seemingly blessed life. There were wonderful things about it no doubt. Yet, deep within me was this internal fist that, if I could have put words to it, was saying, 'I fulfilled my part of the bargain, God. Now, *you* fulfill yours.' It was nothing more than a contract. It had nothing to do with my love for God or my desire to know him for that matter. So, it had to be dismantled. *I* had to be dismantled so God could surface what I was working so hard to keep hidden. You see, God wanted so much more for me. He is always working to give us so much more than we realize is possible. I couldn't be more grateful."

"So all your angry words, your accusations, this was your entitled spirit surfacing?"

"Yes."

"God wanted your fist to surface?"

"Yes, again."

"In fact, he was orchestrating this to some degree?"

"Yes, to some degree."

After a long, ruminating pause, Joe asked, "You mentioned that there was much more God wanted to give. Can you put more words to what you mean?"

Job took a lingering sip of his coffee. Joe decided to do the same. He waited with bated breath to hear what he was going to say.

"He wanted to give me hope. But hope needed to be redefined for me. It wasn't God who needed to see the entitlement in my heart. He sees everything hidden within us. It was me, Joseph. I needed to see what was in my heart. When I finally saw my sense of deep entitlement, something shifted. The Spirit of God could now find room to dwell within me. I began to see God for who he really is, not the false God I had made him out to be. It led to a change of direction for me, a movement toward life, a movement toward God, which at the same time was a movement away from who I used to be, and the false understandings that used to drive my life."

"So he was working for the good."

"He is always working for the good. Even when it doesn't feel that way."

Job took another bite of his brownie. "Do you remember what I said to God when my heart had shifted toward him?"

"For my ears have heard of you, but now my eyes have seen you." Joe quoted it from memory.

"Yes. My eyes were finally open. It was a radical change from the inside out. I finally began to know God. Knowing him better made all the difference."

"It also led you to repentance? At least that is the word you used, didn't you? 'I repent in dust and ashes.'"

"Yes, it did. Yet, repentance is so badly misunderstood. It is normally understood as trying to force someone to do something that they don't really want to do. Like telling a raging alcoholic 'Stop drinking.' Or telling a chain smoker 'Stop smoking.' As if they could summon up the will to just change. Even if they could, behavioral change doesn't go deep enough. Real change has to do with facing our misconceptions of God. It is relational change that God is after. To repent is to move toward life, to move toward God, which means moving away from our false understandings of God. Deep down that's what we really want the most. At least those of us who want to know God personally. It's quite hopeful."

With that, Joe leaned back in his chair and let out a heaving breath that dissolved all the tension he was feeling. He was at rest in a new way and marveled at what a good conversation could do in someone's heart. He took off his boat shoes, stretched his legs out, and put his feet on the hearth of the fireplace.

They lingered a long time in silence, finishing their desserts and enjoying the hot coffee.

"May I ask you another question?" Joe asked as he stared into the fire.

"Be my guest, Joseph."

"At the beginning of the book of Job, God had a strange conversation with Satan, which seemed to be the catalyst for all that went wrong in your life. Some would say that God used you as a pawn in a chess match against the devil."

Anticipating where Joe was heading, Job replied, "Yes, Joseph. God did draw Satan into the story, into my story, deliberately. But I wasn't the pawn. If anyone was a pawn, it was the devil. God knew what he had in mind for me, the greatest good available to humanity: to know him personally. Yet for the devil, it was just another example of how God uses all of Satan's evil strategies for his own good purposes. My story was a mere precursor to the final victory won by God the Father as Jesus, God the Son, died on the cross for the sins of the world. The cross is the final victory, and the resurrection is the celebration of that victory."

Joe sat up in his chair and thought about saying "Amen!" but wanted to express his sense of exuberance in a way that didn't sound so spiritual. He was fed up with spiritual-sounding words, especially the ones he often hid behind. Joe thought about it for a while and finally said, "Way to go, God!" and put up his hand in order to give Job a high five.

Joe was confused when Job's hands remained folded on the table. At first he thought Job did not understand this modern form of celebration. But then the look on Job's face confused him even more. Job leaned forward and with a look of deep concern said, "Joe, are you all right? Are you okay, Joe?" Job placed both hands on Joe's shoulders and gently shook him. "Are you okay, Joe? I'm right here. Can you see me, Joe? You're okay. I'm right here."

Before Joe could say a word, his eyes refocused, and he found himself back in his hospital bed at Bright Star nursing home, gazing into the eyes of Dalia, who had come by to give him a shower earlier than expected.

FIVE
A WOUND REVEALED

She gave this name to the LORD who spoke to her:
"You are the God who sees me," for she said,
"I have now seen the One who sees me."
- Genesis 16:13, NIV

"Joe, can you hear me?" said Dalia.

He nodded his head in the affirmative.

"Whoa, you had me more than a bit worried. You were talking with your eyes closed. You seemed to be having a conversation with someone, but I'm the only one in the room."

In his now characteristically weak voice, he replied, "It's a long story, Dalia."

"Well, I've got the time if you want to share," she said with an inviting tone.

"You wouldn't believe me if I told you."

"Try me," she said with a warm smile.

"OK. Don't say I didn't warn you. But before I do . . . why are you here early? It's only Wednesday morning."

"I had time and wanted to see my favorite patient."

"Oh . . . well . . . I don't know about that."

She leaned closer to him, "It's true Joe."

"Ok. I believe you. Thanks. You promise you won't laugh at what I am about to tell you?"

"I promise, Joe," said Dalia as she crossed her heart.

"Well, it seems God is doing some important work in me, here, near the end of my earthly journey. In the last day or so I've had conversations with two people who no longer inhabit this planet. They are now, well, they are . . ." He hesitated to go on for fear of sounding even more crazy.

The room grew silent enough for them to hear the ticking clock, which hung unobtrusively on the back wall near the bay window, the window Joe had catapulted through not too long ago.

"Go on," Dalia said softly.

"They are now . . . citizens of heaven."

Silence filled the room, and the ticking clock sounded to Joe more like a ticking bomb sure to explode in a way that would cause Dalia to laugh at his ridiculously wild experiences.

Yet, Dalia was looking down. She seemed to be pondering Joe's words. Her gaze never left the floor, and then her eyebrows lifted as if she had a moment of illumination.

Then she finally replied, "Oh."

"Oh?" Joe replied, wondering if he had said too much.

"I mean, oh that's quite something," answered Dalia awkwardly.

To his own surprise, Joe let the silence build between them. He remembered Job's words about following the rhythm of the Holy Spirit. He knew he was often guilty of filling the silence with a joke or a Bible verse. He was learning that silence, however unnerving, was also like the backdrop of an artist's canvas. It provided space for the Spirit of God to create something beautiful.

After a while, Dalia spoke. "Joe?" she sheepishly replied.

"Yes?"

"I'm recalling your spiritual story . . . and I'm so thankful you shared it with me. But, to be honest, the thought of eternity kinda scares me."

"I appreciate you sharing that with me. Do you think you could you put words to why it scares you?" As he said those words, Joe wondered if he was getting close to hearing about her wound.

"Well, I just can't imagine living forever. There was a time when it intrigued me. But now, well, it seems so ominous. It's almost easier to believe that we will just cease to exist when we die."

"Huh," Joe said. He was quite aware in the moment that he did not know how to proceed. Dalia was opening her soul to him. The sacredness of the moment was palpable. It was as if he were walking around a castle, a castle that was her soul. He could also perceive by the tone in her voice that there was a moat around the castle warding off all those who attempted to enter. Yet now, quite spontaneously, her disclosure of fear was like an open window in the castle. It was a small window, to be sure, but an important window nonetheless. Joe quickly became aware that this open window was a deep gesture of trust. There was a sacred weight to her words, as if he was holding a glass jar filled with precious jewels.

"Oh, um. Thanks for trusting me with that," he said clumsily, aware that he was out of his depth. "I'm not sure, but it seems to me that your fear concerning eternity might be something worth exploring. Would you agree?"

"Hmm," she said as she pulled the soap and sponge for his shower out of her bag, placing them beside her. "I think I do agree. No one has ever put it that way before. On top of that, no one has ever been curious enough to ask."

"My goodness, what a shame."

Tears began to well up in her eyes. Joe, sensing a pause within himself, allowed those words to sink in. He was surprised by how well he was tagging along with the Holy Spirit. *Hey, I think I'm getting the hang of this.* He quietly repented of that statement, knowing instinctively that those words could not have come from the Holy Spirit, but were more than likely energized by his pride. He closed his eyes. *My goodness, this relational conversation stuff is difficult. Pride seems to slip in so easily.*

"Watcha thinking, Joe?"

He thought for a moment of telling her what just transpired in his mind but then thought better of it, perceiving that the internal lesson was more for him than for her.

"Just thinking, Dalia. I am curious about why eternity feels ominous to you. Would you mind putting words to it if you can?"

Joe could see the wheels turning in her mind as if she was sifting through her mental memory banks for when she first began to feel this way. She closed her eyes as if making a connection. Then she opened her eyes, looking up at the ceiling. She was breathing rapidly.

Joe went with a hunch. "Are you recalling a story?"

Without a word, she put her finger on the tip of her nose as she fought back tears.

"Dalia, as you recall the story, please know that you are under no obligation to share it with me. Just know that I'm willing to listen."

She took a deep breath and then exhaled. "It might sound silly to you."

"Is that how you view it . . . as silly?"

"Yes, I do, and actually no, I do not."

"Seems conflicting."

"Yes, that's a perfect word for it . . . conflicting. It brings up conflicting emotions."

A long silent pause ensued between them, and then Dalia began to share the story. "I was ten years old sitting in the front row at my grandfather's funeral. He had died suddenly at the age of eighty-three of an aneurysm. He was a very gentle man when he was alive. I loved being around him. He made me feel incredibly special. It was as if he could see me, ya know? I knew that he had some sort of belief in the afterlife, but we never really got around to talking about it. He had a quiet sort of faith. He enjoyed reading his small leather Bible. I would see him with it every so often. It puzzled me a bit. 'Why would he want to read *that* book?' I would think to myself. Most of the adults I knew read the newspaper or magazines about celebrities and current events. He didn't talk much about his faith, but I could tell it was real. I wanted to know more; I just didn't know how to ask. It's not the sort of thing you just bring up in casual conversation. Anyway, I could never muster up the courage. Then after he died, well, it was too late. That quiet hunger seemed to die, or so I thought, along with my grandfather. There I sat, in front of his open casket. His lifeless body just lying there. Every once in a while, it looked like he was taking a breath. I'd lean in to see if someone had made a mistake, hoping they had. I was wrong. He was gone. I had never experienced anything that seemed so final as death. *His* death."

They sat quietly. To Joe, her openness seemed pregnant with new possibilities. After the silence lingered for a while, he followed another hunch. "Is there more?"

As Dalia quietly gazed at Joe, this time with a slight smile, she again put her finger to her nose. Then Dalia continued. "After the funeral, I went back to my house with my family. We hosted a time for people to come over, share in some appetizers, and offer condolences. I heard a lot of different things from people. 'Your grandfather loved you, Dalia.' 'It'll take time, but you'll get over this, Dalia.' 'Your grandfather would want you to get on with your life, Dalia.' They were all well-meaning of course. The thing is, I didn't want to move on. I didn't want to get over it. It felt as if most of them were hastily putting flowers around his grave when I still had a shovel in it. It was more than just a matter of grieving his loss, that was certainly true. I wanted to understand what he knew. Was he still alive somewhere? Or was I just silly for even asking such a question? It was as if most people around me were content with living out their lives in the present without giving much thought about what happens after we die. I was confused and ashamed. Why couldn't I just do the same? Why did I have these looming questions when others seemed not to care one way or another?" Dalia glanced at

Joe, and by the trusting look on her face, he knew she found some rest in having his undivided attention. She pressed through.

"I pulled my mother aside at the house. She was grieving pretty hard. She had just lost her dad. Ya know? But I had this burning question. So, I asked her, 'Mom, where is grandpa now?' She got angry. She briskly wiped the tears from her face and said . . . and said . . ."

Joe waited quietly for her to continue.

"She shouted, 'Dalia, you ask too many questions!' Then she stormed off."

There was silence for a while.

"Oh, my," Joe said. "What was it like hearing those words from your mom?"

She thought about it and said, "It was like the jab of a knife. I learned then that it was dangerous to ask questions. So, I shoved them down within me as far as I could."

Joe nodded and gently said, "I see."

She looked at Joe, waiting for him to say more.

He looked back and said, "Please, continue."

She offered a weak smile and then resumed, "Time went on. Life just kept me busy enough to forget about my burning question. Yet, it seemed the more I ignored it, the more dread it produced in me. Ten years later I decided to do something about it. I went to talk to a relative of a friend of mine who was a religious professor at a nearby college. I had become an acquaintance of his over the years, talked to him at my friend's house a handful of times. To be honest, I wasn't very drawn to him as a person, but I knew he was very intelligent. I was impressed by him, which, now that I think about it, was more like being afraid of him. He seemed to live in a lofty tower, metaphorically speaking. Almost untouchable. A guru on top of a lonely mountain. Surely he could shed some light on my burning question."

She paused and looked hesitantly at Joe.

"Go on. You have my attention."

She let out a sigh of relief, then kept talking.

"I had to set up an appointment with him. It seemed there were quite a few people clamoring to spend some time on the proverbial mountain top. He seemed to have arrived at a balanced life, which I desperately wanted but always found illusive. When I finally got to his office, he was sitting behind his large oak desk. I sat down in a chair on the other side of the desk, facing him. The desk gave the impression of an iceberg separating my little life boat from the promise of solid ground. The whole setting felt quite foreboding." She leaned forward, putting her elbows on her knees and grasping her hands together.

"'Hi, Professor Chesil,' I said. He barely looked up from the papers he was grading. With what I perceived to be a forced smile, he said, 'Hi, Dalia. What can I do for you?' He was quick and to the point. I had the distinct impression I was bothering him. But he did not say that explicitly. It was more felt by, I think, the energy of his words, if that makes sense to you? He was politely distant. Strangely, this strengthened the allure of the ivory tower. I wanted to be there. I wanted to feel as if I had arrived, just like him. I felt ashamed that I might be wasting his time, so I decided to jump right into my question."

Joe interjected. "Given how you were feeling, and what you experienced from your mother, that took some real courage to continue."

"Thanks. Although I felt more desperate than courageous."

"Fair enough. I think I know what you mean," Joe said tenderly.

She nodded with a smile and then continued. "'Professor, I've been struggling with a question ever since my grandpa died ten years ago,' I said. 'He had an understanding of eternity that, to him, was very real. Yet, it seems that most people I encounter are focused on this life and either don't have time to think about eternity or simply have no desire to do so. But I do. Mainly because of my grandpa. He seemed to exude a kind of peace that transcended this world. I presume, with you being a religious professor, you might have insights for me? I thought you might help shed some light on my struggle.' Then I sat back in my chair and waited for his reply."

Joe interjected again, "Do you remember how you were feeling in that moment?"

"Unburdened and nervous all at the same time."

"Other than your mother, was he the first one with whom you shared your struggle?"

"Yes."

"Yet, even though you bared your soul, for some reason you didn't feel safe with him?"

"Yes again," she replied.

Joe grabbed his bed rail and attempted to pull himself a bit closer to her. He had a sense what was coming wasn't good and wanted her to know that he was listening.

"Professor Chesil looked up from his papers and gave me a smile. Then he came from around his desk and sat in a chair near me. He grabbed my hand and seemed almost genuine. 'My dear Dalia,' he said, 'if believing in eternity works for you that's fine. There's nothing inherently wrong with it. Some people need to believe in an afterlife. Some don't. If it helps you live better while you're alive, that's what really matters, living your best life now! Like your grandfather, you may need to believe that there is something after we die. It might work for you.'

"'Work for me?' I said.

"'Yes. Does it help balance you out in this life now? That's what I mean. Believe what works for you. If it gives you peace, then great. Believe it.'

"'But that doesn't seem to make sense. Either there is life after death or there isn't.'"

She looked up at Joe. "That's when he withdrew his hand and sat back in his chair."

"What happened next?"

"His forced smile came back, and he said, 'So many questions, Dalia. I would rather believe in what I know for sure. *This* life I know. I can see it. I can feel it. To be honest I have never had the need to believe in an afterlife.'

"'The need?' I said.

"'Yes, the need,' Professor Chesil replied.

"'But you're a professor of religion,' I said.

"'True. I look at all religions and glean from them what makes this life work better. I don't give much thought to what comes after we die. Don't take this the wrong way, but most well-adjusted people don't need to believe in an afterlife. Weaker people need to believe in eternity. It is a kind of crutch to lean on. It can be helpful in giving people some strength to be productive citizens in the here and now. I don't fault anyone who believes in an afterlife. Dalia, if it helps you, if believing in eternity somehow comforts you, then go right ahead. Believe what gives you comfort and peace. You have the freedom to believe whatever you want.

You wouldn't be the first one to do so, and you certainly won't be the last.'"

Dalia paused from the story to catch her breath. She looked at Joe. "To say that I was staggered by his words would be an understatement. I had no idea how to respond. His words seemed kind yet with a strange twist."

"Like another jab of a knife?"

She looked at Joe. "Yes," she said quietly. "What he said confirmed what I most feared: The desire to understand what came after this life was silly and emerged from my screwed-up, insecure life. I sat there paralyzed by shame and fear.

"Then Professor Chesil said abruptly, 'Anything else, Dalia? I do have papers to correct. You understand, I'm sure.'

"I think he was sincerely trying to help me, Joe, but it didn't come across that way. I quickly said, 'No, huh, thanks for your time.' Then got out of there as fast as I could. I decided to keep the question buried. It seemed best at the time. Since then a sense of dread has followed me like a lion crouching in the tall grass ready to pounce. Self-chastisement seemed to work well enough. 'Stop being so silly, Dalia. Stop being so needy, Dalia. Your questions are stupid, Dalia. Just forget about them, Dalia. They'll only get you in trouble, Dalia,' I would say to myself. As best as I could, I just kept getting on with my life. But the thirst to understand, coupled with the sense of dread, have remained."

"That's quite a story," Joe said with kind affection. "Have you ever shared this with anyone else?"

"No. I haven't. You're the first."

"Well then, I feel very honored that you would share it with me."

Her eyes welled up with tears again as she fought to hold back the floodgates.

More out of curiosity than anything else, Joe asked, "What's it like to finally share that story?"

Dalia took a long time to respond. "It feels like something is being unlocked. A door that has remained locked for a long, long time. The thing is, Joe, and this is a very strange thing to think about, it feels as though I'm the one who has kept the door locked from the inside, until this moment right now. I guess I needed someone curious enough to stand near the door, to gently wonder about what was on the other side."

"Isn't that something," Joe said, who was just as amazed by this as Dalia seemed to be. They both sat wonderstruck by what had just transpired between them.

"Can I ask you one more question?" Joe said.

"Sure. Please do."

"What are you feeling right now? I mean, are you feeling the dread that has followed you all these years? Is the crouching lion still lurking in the tall grass?"

She took considerable time to answer this question and then replied, "Actually, yes. But now there seems to be a difference."

"What might that difference be?"

"I don't feel the need to run from it anymore. I think I might be able to find the courage to turn around and stare it in the face. While that feels like death to me, perhaps it will not result in death after all? Maybe the answer, or at least part of the answer, will emerge as I confront that which I have feared for so long. What would you say to that, Joe?"

"I would say that seems counterintuitive. But then again,

most truths are counterintuitive. I'm so glad for you. I will be very curious as to where all of this leads you."

"Believe me, you'll be the first to know." Dalia looked down at the soap and sponge next to her bag. "Now, I think it is time for your shower. What do you think, Joe? Are you up for it?" she said with some lightness in her voice.

Joe sighed and with a resigned smile said, "OK. Let's get it done."

She gently touched his forearm, holding his gaze for a few moments. "Thanks for enduring my ramblings."

"It was an honor listening to you. Believe me, I wasn't enduring anything. I very much enjoyed listening to you. You had me spellbound. If those are your ramblings, then feel free to ramble anytime. Really. I would love to carry on the conversation. Can we put a comma after this time rather than a period?"

With tears welling up in her eyes again, Dalia said, "I would love that, Joe."

"To be continued, then?" Joe added.

"To be continued," she replied. Dalia proceeded to get Joe into his wheelchair and then onto a plastic chair in the shower where she took her time washing him from head to toe. After she dried him well, she dressed him and gently helped him back into his hospital bed. As she was packing up her things, he noticed a catalog of some kind in her medical bag.

"Doing some shopping, Dalia?" He gestured with his eyes to the catalog.

"Oh yes, actually. A friend of mine loves candles, and I came across this incredible one just the other day. Look at it, Joe. Three people, each holding a candle . . . and they're dancing! Isn't it absolutely beautiful?"

Joe gazed intently at the picture. With his thirst igniting and his voice quivering, he replied, "More than words can say, Dalia. More than words can say."

As she gathered her things, she looked back at Joe and said, "See you next Tuesday, my friend, for a companion visit."

Joe, again caught up in the reality of things, said, "I look forward to it, Dalia." Feeling exhausted from his shower, he closed his eyes and went to sleep.

SIX

LOVE, GRACE, FELLOWSHIP

*The point is that Christian experience of God in its
entirety, including worship, prayer, or what have you, is
inescapably Trinitarian. How often have you
heard that taught, preached, or stressed?*
- Robert Letham, The Holy Trinity

I t was a warm summer day. There was a gentle breeze
blowing in the air. The sun was bright and illuminated a
dirt path before him. To Joe's surprise, he found himself
walking. He looked around dumbfounded, having no
recollection of how he came to be in this extraordinary place.
He remembered his conversation with Dalia. He also
remembered closing his eyes for a nap as he pondered the
reality at the center of all things. *What a beautiful way to fall
asleep.*

Looking down at himself, Joe realized that he was back
in his thirty-year-old body. *It seems I am back in liminal*

space. I wonder what this time will hold for me. All I know is that it's so good to be walking again. To feel the muscles and sinews in my legs stretching and contracting with each stride? Incredible!

He lifted his eyes and saw a multitude of trees: oak trees, willow trees, fruit trees, and more, on either side of the path. Birds chirped melodiously as they flew overhead. He bent down to touch the dirt path. Grabbing a handful of dirt, he picked it up and, like an hourglass, let it cascade through his fingers. As he brushed his hands off, Joe looked up and saw a cherry tree. He went over to it, picked a cherry off, looked it over, and then placed it in his mouth. It was subtly tart and sour, and there was also a juicy sweetness to it. He took the pit from between his lips and threw it onto a dirt patch near some other trees. To his amazement, it immediately sprouted. He took a deep breath in. *Lilacs!* Turning around, he saw the purple bushes lining the left side of the path behind him. *Maria loved lilacs.* He took another deep breath in, savoring the smell.

As he walked, he looked around wide-eyed. Flowers were in full bloom on each side of the path: chrysanthemums, peonies, sunflowers, zinnias, and many more. He took another look at the trees on either side of the path, which were resplendent in color and stature.

Joe walked for what seemed like an hour. He didn't know for sure because he did not have a watch. This felt liberating to him, and he wondered about heaven, where time was no longer something to be measured but rather something to be relished and enjoyed. *Perhaps in heaven there is no such thing as time at all? Perhaps in heaven there is only the eternal now?* Thoughts like these stirred his thinking as to what grand surprises lay ahead of him in the city yet to come.

Joe was so caught up in his thoughts that he was startled by the man who quietly came up alongside him. He was a short man with dark-brown shoulder-length hair that complemented his dark-brown eyes. The man wore a simple button-down white linen shirt, untucked, which stretched across his rather large upper torso. The buttons on his shirt looked like each were made of a single pearl. He wore dark-green linen shorts revealing his legs, which appeared to be built like tree trunks.

"Aren't they incredible?" said the man who seemed to be asking a rhetorical question.

Joe was confused at first as he looked around with some bewilderment. By following the man's gaze, Joe realized he was talking about the flowers.

"Ah yes, of course! The flowers. They are truly incredible." While Joe didn't yet know this man's identity, he was grateful to share an appreciation for the beautiful creation surrounding them.

After a while Joe asked, "Do I know you by any chance?"

"You might know me, at least by name. I lived on earth a bit before your time. But some of my writings, by the grace and wisdom of God, endured on earth after I crossed the threshold into heaven."

"May I ask? What is your name?"

"It's John," said the man as they continued to stroll together down the dirt path. "Names are so important, aren't they, Joseph? They speak to a uniqueness about us. They touch upon our personal history. How can we begin to truly know people without first knowing their names?"

"I guess you're right. Although, I haven't given it all that much thought."

They walked a while longer in silence. Betting on a hunch, Joe said, "John?"

"Yes, Joseph?"

"You seem to be the kind of man who actually *notices* people."

The man smiled. "What a compliment, Joseph. Thank you for those words. You might be interested to know that all those in heaven notice each other. Uniqueness is celebrated there, largely because everyone in heaven reveals something unique about God."

Joe let that thought sink in. "That's mind-blowing," he said as he placed his hands on his temples, expanding his fingers outward as he spoke.

"Yes, it is," John said while mimicking the same hand gesture. "It never gets old, Joseph. The sheer wonder and awe of it never winds down. It's as if there is one discovery after another after another. Relationships never tire there, if you can imagine."

"That's about all I can do right now. Imagine. You know, since you have lived on earth yourself, that there is a widespread lack of curiosity about other people. It seems that we are all self-obsessed. We try so hard to make an impression on others we have no space left to allow others to make an impression on us."

"You include yourself, Joseph?"

"To some degree, sadly, I do."

They walked in silence for a while.

"That's a very good sign," said John.

This startled Joe a bit and intrigued him even more. He replied, "Can you elaborate on that a bit?"

"You are aware of how subtle sin can be in your own soul and how it damages others. Deep down, self-obsession, lack of curiosity about others, are relational sins, because they harm people. The fact that you can see the plank in your own eye is good. It helps you to be gracious when you see the sliver in the eyes of others. Those who are more troubled about the hurtful ways they relate are prone to offer grace because they know they are guilty of the same thing. It makes you safe. It makes you trustworthy."

"Safe and trustworthy." Joe repeated the words. "I hope that has been the case. I guess I'll take your word for it."

"You can take it all the way to the bank," replied John as he smiled at Joe.

Some more time passed.

"I see Christ in you, Joseph," John said in almost a whisper.

Joe teared up. "Really? You haven't known me for very long. I'm so glad you see Him in me. I couldn't get a better compliment. Thank you."

"You're very welcome," said John.

They strolled along until they saw a long wooden picnic table with benches on each side. It was situated on the right side of the path, resting on a patch of lush green grass. They went over to it and sat down, one on each side so they were facing each other. Joe's back was to the path.

"You said your name is John. You're not the apostle John? Are you? You said you did some writing that endured? Were you actually one of the authors in the Bible?"

"I think you mean one of the coauthors Joseph?" said the man, feigning inquiry but asking rhetorically.

"Ah yes, coauthor with the Holy Spirit. Yes, good catch.

We should really give the Holy Spirit credit where credit is due. I think he might appreciate that."

This made John laugh in a deep tone that seemed to shake the trees on either side of the path. When his laugh subsided, he addressed Joe's question.

"The apostle John? I'm glad you mentioned him! I loved his sacred letters. He wrote with such biblical imagination, with the Holy Spirit guiding each word. His letters are wonderful, and I enjoy the man even more! What a unique human being! He reveals Jesus in such a beautiful way!"

"Oh, so you're not him then," Joe said with a bit of disappointment in his voice. "I'm sure he's quite popular in heaven. I can only imagine how many people wait in line for a chance to talk to him."

"There are no lines in heaven, Joseph. Since we have all of eternity to meet people, no one is in a hurry. So, there is no need for lines."

Joe tried hard to imagine this, but it proved difficult. "I guess I'll know it when I see it. And besides, while you're not as important as the apostle John, it sure is nice talking with you."

He realized immediately how condescending that must have sounded. Stumbling over his words, he tried to backtrack. "What I really meant to say was . . . he was an apostle . . . and you're . . . well . . . you're just you . . . well not just you . . . you're you . . . and you're important in your own way. Ya know what I mean?" Wishing he could vanish, he lowered his head. *Why don't you get yourself a shovel, Joe. This hole seems to be getting deeper by the second.*

When Joe lifted his head, he saw tears welling up in John's eyes and a look of peace that could calm a raging sea. "Be at rest, Joseph. I know what you mean. I take no offense.

Self-importance is no longer a problem for those in heaven. I'm delighted to step aside for the apostle John. He would do the same for me."

With those words, Joe realized that, in John, there was no hint of insecurity to be found. No anger. No wringing of the hands. No wishing that he was somebody else. No indication at all of being offended. In that moment, Joe longed to be entirely *himself*.

"It's good to have this opportunity to walk down the road with you a bit, Joseph."

"Yes, this sure is a beautiful path, wherever it is. I don't think I've ever walked a road so beautiful," he said as he looked around taking in the sights once more.

"Ah yes, this road is absolutely beautiful. But as you also now know, you've been walking another road. One that is not always easy to see. The work God does for us on the salvation road stretches into eternity."

"Oh yes, right, of course. The salvation road. How could I forget! So, you're here to help me move down the salvation road a bit more?" Joe asked.

"Not so much to help you move down the road. That's God work. I'm here to walk alongside you, to discover with you what God is up to in your life right now in the radical present. Every moment, every detail of your life is used by God to mature you into the man you are destined to be. I'm sure you have heard the phrase 'the devil is in the details'? It's actually the other way around Joseph, God is the one who is in the details. With God, nothing in your life goes to waste. Every success, every failure, every moment of happiness, every season of suffering . . . it is all used by God to get you ready for the eternal dance."

With an upward tilt of the head, John looked over Joe's

shoulder. When Joe turned around, there on the other side of the path was the three-person candelabra thoughtfully placed on an ivory stand. Each candle—royal purple, crimson red, and the pure white of a dove —was lit, and the candelabra, like before, was rotating. Joe's holy thirst awakened.

"The Father loves you, Joseph," said John affectionately.

"I know God loves me. I really do," Joe said longingly.

"Actually, what I mean to say is that the Father has his own unique and personal love for you."

That caught Joe off guard. "Say what now?"

"Do you remember the words of Jesus? 'In that day you will ask in my name, and I do not say I will ask the Father on your behalf, for the Father himself loves you, because you have loved me and have believed that I came from God.' It is the Father's special attitude toward you, love."

"But wait a minute," Joe retorted. "Doesn't Jesus also love me? And the Holy Spirit, he is the love of God poured into me. Am I correct?"

"Yes, that's true. All three persons love you in a unique way. You are loved by the Father with a fatherly love. You are loved by Jesus with the love of a Savior and a friend. You are loved by the Holy Spirit as the one who comes alongside you and makes you aware of your belovedness. All I simply want to do is point out that the Father loves you uniquely with a fatherly love, with warmth, tenderness, and great affection. You may be surprised to find out that the word 'love' in the Bible is attributed most to the Father. Love is distinctly ascribed to him."

"Can that really be true?" Joe said with astonishment.

"Here's a verse that most people overlook, 'For God so

loved the world that he gave his only Son, that whoever believes in him should not perish but have eternal life.'"

They sat in silence until Joe said, "I'm not sure what you're getting at."

"Jesus was talking about his Father. It was God the Father who loved the world and gave his only begotten Son. Jesus loved talking about his Father. Still does!"

"Oh wow. I don't think I've ever seen that before."

"How about this one, 'See what kind of love the Father has given us, that we should be called the children of God, and so we are.'"

"Oh, that's so good!" Joe could feel his heart melting. "I'm amazed by this! I really am!"

"So am I, Joseph. So am I. It's a truth that never gets old and only expands with meaning."

They got up from the bench and walked on for a while in silence.

"There is such an easy and unforced way about you, John," Joe said, breaking the silence.

"God's Trinitarian life pulsates in me. It's made all the difference. God is a relationship of three. There is nothing forced by the way they relate to each other. God has transformed me into a truly relational being by offering, inviting, but never coercing. He's doing the same in you, Joe, as you travel the salvation road."

"That's such a beautiful thought. Thanks for sharing. To hear that the Father has a unique love for me touches something deep inside."

"I'm glad," replied John, as he placed his hand on Joe's back.

They strolled on for a while.

"Jesus loves being your Savior, Joseph," John said affectionately.

"Wait, can you say that again?"

"Jesus loves being your Savior."

Joe took some time to ruminate on those words. "I know he loves me, but I don't know if I've ever heard that he loves being my Savior."

"New thought then?"

"I think so," Joe said, scratching his head.

"Jesus is the only person within the Trinity who became a human being. He knows what it is like to live in the fallen world. He lived, suffered, and died, just as we live, suffer, and die. He knows how it feels in the most intimate way. He is and forever will be God in human flesh, fully God and fully man."

"Some say that Jesus is a mixture of God and man. Still others say that Jesus is part God and part man. And still others say that Jesus is two people, one human and one divine. I've always felt cautious about those views."

"As you should, my lad. Herein lies the great mystery of grace, the grace of *union* within Jesus. He is fully God and fully man, not a mixture of the two, nor just a part of each, and not two people. He is *one* person. He is fully man so he could fully represent us. He is fully God so he could fully redeem us."

As John spoke, Joe thought he heard the smallest hint of a British accent.

"So if love is mostly attributed to the Father, what is mostly attributed to Jesus?"

John stopped and knelt down to gently touch a white lily growing on the left side of the path. "And from his fullness we have all received grace upon grace."

"That's in chapter one of John's gospel," Joe said.

"Yes. So the answer to your question is grace," John said as he stood back up and smiled at Joe.

"I've always loved that verse," he said as he looked at John.

They stood there gazing at each other. "Do you remember what Jesus said to the apostle Paul when he asked Jesus to take away his thorn in the flesh?"

Joe spoke from memory. "My grace is sufficient for you for my power is made perfect in weakness."

Now, Joe bent down to look at the lily. "I've always loved that verse too."

"Why so?"

Joe had to think for a moment. Looking back up at John, he replied, "I guess because it takes the pressure off. It's the opposite of the try-harder message." As he said those words, Joe was aware that the bond between them was deepening. They were becoming, in their short time together, soul friends.

Just ahead of them, they saw a dove perched on what appeared to be the branch of an olive tree.

"I suppose you're going to talk about the Holy Spirit now?"

"Yes," John said as they looked at the dove. He continued, "The Holy Spirit deepens your desire for the Father and the Son."

"I know from the Apostle's Creed that the Holy Spirit proceeds from the Father and the Son."

"Yes, Joseph. He joins us into fellowship with them. Love is most attributed to the Father, grace is most attributed to the Son, fellowship is most attributed to the Holy Spirit.

He brings us into fellowship with the Father and the Son. He deepens that fellowship."

"What a beautiful thought. From what you just said, I'm struck by the fact that God shares who he is with us. Not that we become part of God, but that God in the form of the Holy Spirit is their shared love . . . and now they have shared their love with us."

"What a great thought! God loves to share. It's in his very nature. That's why we were created. God wanted to share his life with us. God did not create us because he was lonely or needy. He created us out of his fullness because he loves to share all that he has, all that he is!"

"So unlike us. We tend to keep good things for ourselves."

"Yet, now that the Holy Spirit lives in us, our desires have been transformed. Deep down we truly want to share what God has given to us with others."

"So, love is the characteristic of the Father. Grace is the characteristic of the Son. Fellowship is the characteristic of the Holy Spirit. Love, Grace, Fellowship."

"Now you're getting it. We can know all three persons of the Trinity in unique ways. It's right there in the last verse of Paul's second letter to the Corinthians, 'The grace that comes through our Lord Jesus Christ, the love that is of God the Father, and the fellowship that is ours in the Holy Spirit be with you all!'"

"I don't think I ever saw that before."

"They are distinct in another way. The Father begets, or eternally births, the Son. The Son is begotten, or is eternally birthed, from the Father. The Holy Spirit proceeds, or is eternally breathed out, from the Father and the Son."

Joe bent down to pick up a smooth stone. As he held it in

his hand, he said, "This is touching something very deep in me, John. I don't entirely know why, but it feels like it is touching the very center of me."

"Perhaps because the Holy Spirit dwells in your very center?"

"Yes, perhaps."

They stopped near a pulsing stream on the left side of the path. Joe took the smooth stone and skipped it across the water. "Your words carry so much weight, John. You truly have a pastor's heart."

"It's my pleasure to have walked with you a bit. I look forward to seeing you again."

"Oh, we're done so soon?"

"There are others you are meant to meet before you cross the threshold. But we will see each other again in a little while. I promise."

"I look forward to it so much."

They gazed at the stream together.

Joe heard the swish, swish, swish of the stream as it seemed to pulsate with a certain rhythm. He suddenly felt a bit woozy. He shut his eyes and stretched out his arms to maintain balance.

He opened his eyes to the pulsing sound of his oxygen concentrator pumping O_2 into the long plastic hose, which flowed through the cannula placed in his nostrils. He was back in his hospital bed at Bright Star nursing home. Then in a flash of illumination, Joe's eyes widened. *Oh my goodness, I think I was talking with John Owen.*

SEVEN
FACING THE LION

Christians who do not have the feeling that
they must flee the crucified Christ have probably not yet
understood him in a sufficiently radical way.
- Jürgen Moltmann, The Crucified God

J oe lay still in his bed, partly because it proved more and more difficult for him to move. Yet, the stillness was deeper than the mere physical. *What a wonderful time with John Owen.* As soon as he said those words, like a python, the darkness began slithering toward him, threatening to choke out all that was good. Joe started to quake with fear. As he gripped his bed rails for dear life, the questions came flooding back to his mind, taunting him. *What good is my life? Have I ever made a difference in anyone's journey? What use am I? Does God care? Is God real? If he's real, then why does his presence elude me? Why am I more aware of his felt absence than his felt presence?*

Psalm 139 came to his mind. "If I say, 'Surely the darkness shall cover me, and the light about me be night,' even the darkness is not dark to you; the night is bright as the day, for darkness is as light with you." His body relaxed a little, and he loosened his tight grip on the bed rails. His pounding heart slowed. His breathing calmed. *God is with me. Yes, he is with me right here in the darkness.* He remembered Nonna's words, "The darkness does not define you." As he rehearsed those words in his mind, the terrifying questions began to lose their hold. The words of Psalm 139, like a helium balloon, began to expand, pushing the darkness out to the peripheries.

He remembered his conversation with John Owen, how he could know each person of the Trinity in a unique way. As he pondered this, a song began to surface in his heart. This ever-growing relational understanding of God began to slowly reverberate into every fissure and corner of his soul.

Joe recalled how, in the book of the Revelation, the Christians in heaven gathered around the throne singing, "Holy, holy, holy is the Lord God almighty who was, and is, and is to come." *Holy, holy, holy is sung three times. Huh. That couldn't be a coincidence. One for each person of the Trinity. Oh wow! I've never seen that before! All those Christians, caught up in God's immeasurable worth.*

As his mind lingered, imagining the throng of Christians singing those words, Joe forgot about himself. Imperceptibly, he was shifting from self-obsession to God-obsession. He whispered the words of the song over and over again. As he did, his soul found its center. Closing his eyes, he lifted his weak and trembling hands with palms up, repeating the words, *Holy, holy, holy is the Lord God almighty. Who was and is and is to come!*

Over the next several days Joe was sleeping quite a bit. Yet, when he awoke those words would come rushing back to him and he would recite them again. *Holy, holy, holy is the Lord God almighty. Who was and is and is to come!*

While he was quietly mouthing the words, he saw Dalia standing at the door of his room.

"Hi, Joe."

The sight of her warmed Joe's heart, and he couldn't help but smile. "Oh, Dalia. So good to see you. Is it Tuesday already?"

"Yes, it was a quick five days."

"Sure was! But I'm so glad," he said.

"What were you reciting?"

"Oh, you heard me?"

"Yes."

"How long were you standing there?"

"Just a few minutes"

Joe could tell by the wary look on her face that she was a bit unsettled. "Oh, I was reciting the words of a song from the last book of the Bible."

"Really? I didn't know there were songs in the Bible."

"In a very real sense, Dalia, the entire Bible is one extraordinary song, one that God has been singing since he created the world."

"That's a beautiful thought, Joe. I would love to hear more." She looked into her large bag and pulled out her phone along with a small Bluetooth speaker.

Holding her phone in her hand, she said, "Do you mind if I put on some soothing sounds? Just waves gently washing up on a seashore. I can put it on real low so it doesn't interfere with our conversation."

"I'd enjoy that. I have always loved the beach."

"I know it's been getting harder for you to speak with your voice weakening and all. You sure you are up for talking? I could come back another time for a companionship visit. We could talk then."

"Nothing would make me happier than to continue our conversation now."

In a soft tone, Dalia replied, "Thank you, my friend."

"Believe me it's my pleasure. I would love to hear any lingering thoughts from when we spoke last. Or if you want to go in a different direction, that would be fine too." Remembering his conversation with Job about the radical present, Joe sought to meet Dalia in the moment and decided to ask another question. "But before you start talking, let me ask, what's going on in you at this precise moment?"

"What's going on in me?" she said with some bewilderment.

"Yes. I've learned from some special people that it's often good to put words to what we sense internally in the moment."

"I don't think anyone has ever asked me that question. Honestly, I don't think I've ever thought about what is going on inside of me in the present moment, much less try to put words to it in the presence of another person," she said with hesitant awe.

"Believe me, you're not alone. You don't have to answer the question if you don't want to. No pressure. Just an invitation. It certainly doesn't do any good to force someone to think in this direction, but it can be a beautiful thing if someone is willing."

"I'm willing, Joe, but if I am to be honest, I'm a little nervous as well."

"I'd be surprised if you weren't more than a bit nervous. Can you say why?"

"I can try. I don't think it has anything to do with you. I've found you to be a very safe person. Our last conversation solidified that in my heart and mind. I think it has more to do with me. I'm afraid of what I might discover. Will it be too difficult to handle? What will I do with it, once I discover what's going on in me? Will the truth have the power to destroy me? I guess I'm more than a little nervous. Yet, at the same time, I feel a strong desire moving me to discover more about myself. I *want* to find out. I have worked so hard at quelling my questions and fears. I think that's why I've stayed so busy over the years. Quite frankly, it hasn't done me any good. Staying on the surface has kept me living in fear, running from the unknown."

She pondered her own words and then said, "How's that for a start?

"It's a wonderful start, Dalia. You have more courage than you know. It reminds me of something that Jesus once said."

"Please tell me."

"You shall know the truth and the truth shall set you free."

There was a long pause in the discussion. Dalia lowered her head and closed her eyes. It looked like she was doing her best to take in those words. She then lifted her gaze to meet his. "If that's really true, Joe, then I want that freedom. I really do."

"I'm glad." Silent anticipation filled the room again. "So then, would you like to continue?"

"Okay. Here's goes nothing."

"Not nothing, Dalia, *something* truly good. I'm with you

as you share. I long to discover with you what is in your heart. May the Holy Spirit lead us."

She smiled as her shoulders relaxed a bit. "I'd really like to believe there is a Holy Spirit."

"Let's take it one step at a time, shall we?" Joe said reassuringly.

"Okay, so . . . how am I doing in this moment? Let's see. Well, I'm a bit tired. I've had a long day. I've been looking forward to seeing you, and I'm glad that you have the strength to chat with me." She looked at him inquisitively.

"You have my full attention, Dalia."

"Thanks. So, to go a little further, I have this knot in my stomach. I can feel it right now as we speak. If I am honest, and yes, I want to be honest . . . um, if I were to speak truthfully . . . I have lived with this knot in my stomach for a very long time. I've done my best just to live with it. But truth be told, I hate it, and I have no idea what it's about. Well, I may have some idea, since I talked with you last. I'm a runner, Joe, and I've been running for a very long time." She fought back the tears as she let her head drop into her hands.

Several moments went by in silence as Joe did his best to honor those tears. Then Joe finally spoke in a gentle voice. "You're not running now, Dalia."

She breathed out a deep sigh. "That means a great deal to me, Joe," she said as tears welled up her eyes.

"Say more about the knot if you can."

She took a deep breath in and then let it out. "The knot. OK. The knot. Remember when I talked to you about eternity and how it felt so vast and unknown to me? I think I have been running from the unknown. If I'm to be honest, it has terrified me."

A silence filled the room. They exchanged a kind look. Dalia waited for Joe to say something.

Sensing this, Joe spoke, "Maybe acknowledging that terror is a good thing?"

Dalia's face looked puzzled. "That strikes me as odd, but I am strangely drawn to it. Can you say more?"

"Sure. As fallen human beings, we naturally think that feeling internally unsettled must be wrong. So, we work hard at staying balanced. We foolishly think that we should always feel peace. We think we should feel peace about the world around us, peace about the people we relate to, peace about ourselves. On top of that, we don't like feeling unsettled. Even if we somehow believed that experiencing our deep fears was a good thing, we might still run because it is so unnerving to us. We work hard internally. We work hard at staying positive and at peace. We work hard at thinking positive thoughts. We stay busy in order not to feel unsettled. We even pay therapists to help us feel peaceful inside, peace about our world, and peace about ourselves. It may work for a while. It may work for years, even decades. But then something triggers us, and the fears come flooding back. It's like . . ." He searched his mind for a comparison.

"Rearranging furniture on the Titanic?" said Dalia, finishing Joe's sentence for him.

He looked at her with some surprise and then said with a nod, "Why, yes. It is."

"I heard someone use that metaphor once. It just seemed to fit," she said as she shrugged her shoulders and smiled.

"It's a good metaphor . . . it truly, truly is . . . but it's incomplete."

She pondered Joe's words for a while and then asked, "In what sense?"

"We don't have to stay on the Titanic. If we learn to face what is so deeply unsettling to us, there is a lifeboat strong and sure. We don't have to drown in our fears. If we can find a way to *move through* them, we come to understand the life being offered to us. Eternal life."

"Makes sense so far," Dalia said as she mulled over these words. "So then, instead of running from my deep fears, it would be better to acknowledge them? Face them?" she tentatively asked.

"That's a good way of putting it," Joe said, not knowing where she would go with this answer.

After a while she responded, "I think I like what you're saying."

"Can you elaborate?"

"Well, running has simply not worked. I have expended a lot of energy at trying to run. Might as well face my fears."

"Face the lion crouching in the tall grass?" he reminded her.

"Yes. I think so. I want to face the lion."

"I like that, Dalia. That lion just might save your life."

"That sends a shiver down my spine, Joe, but somehow I believe that what you are saying could be true."

She gazed at Joe with a trusting look, which unsettled him a little. Even though he was enjoying the conversation, Joe had no idea what he was doing. *Dear Holy Spirit, I feel woefully unqualified to be speaking with Dalia. If you don't show up, nothing good will happen. I confess my need for you. Please lead me. I'll do my best to tag along.*

Once he finished his silent prayer, the slowly building pressure inside of him eased up a bit. He felt reassured that he didn't need to make anything happen. That was the Holy

Spirit's job. As he sought to fight his own internal battle, Dalia spoke up.

"I found my grandfather's Bible."

"Really?" Joe said in a surprised tone.

"Yes. It was in a box, in my parent's basement. I was looking for something else at the time and happened to stumble upon it. Strange luck, aye, Joe?"

"I'll say," he responded, thinking to himself that it probably wasn't luck at all.

"I was looking through it the other day. My grandfather had highlighted different verses, I guess the ones that stood out to him. I found a real interesting sentence . . . whatever you call it, in some place called Eccl . . . Eccles . . ."

"Ecclesiastes?" Joe chimed in.

"That's the one," said Dalia as she raised a finger in the air. "Difficult to pronounce," she added as she shook her finger slightly.

"Yes, you're right. Not the easiest word to enunciate," He agreed.

Joe then asked, "Well, what did it say?"

She rifled through her bag, taking hold of a notebook where she had written it out. "It says this: 'God has planted eternity in the human heart.' It's as if God did this on purpose, so we could know intuitively that eternity is real."

"And if eternity is real . . ." Joe waited for a response.

"Then God must be real." She completed his sentence. They looked at each other and nodded together.

"Is that the first time you said something like that out loud?"

"Yes, it is. Believe it or not, it stirs something deep inside me."

"Oh, I believe you all right," he said.

"Really? You do?"

"Yes, I do. It's your holy thirst."

"My holy thirst?"

"Yes, it's your thirst for God."

"I didn't know I had a thirst for God. But now that you say so, it does seem to ring true. Wow! I have a thirst for God!" said Dalia like someone opening a gift at Christmas.

"God planted this thirst inside of you so that you could discover your desire for him. Many people never discover this desire and mistake it for something else."

"Amazing . . . I mean . . . this thirst," Dalia replied as the awareness of this discovery seemed to deepen.

"It is amazing, isn't it?" Joe said in harmony.

Then a frown came over Dalia's face.

"What is it, Dalia?"

"I'm glad to discover the thirst, Joe. I really am. It's an incredible discovery, and now I am aware of a longing in me I have never known, but . . ."

"But what?"

"Why do I still feel troubled inside?"

Joe let the question hang in the air for a while. Then he said, "Something's wrong."

Dalia's back stiffened, and her eyes widened. "What's wrong, Joe? Are you okay? Do you need my help in some way?"

"No, no, I'm fine. What I meant was that there is something wrong within you, within all of us. This is part of the reason why you still feel troubled."

She hesitated for a moment as she sat up in her seat. "Please, go on."

"OK I will, since you want me to. Do you remember the candelabra that you bought for your friend?"

"Oh, you mean this one?" She pulled the candelabra out of her large bag.

Joe's eyes widened.

"I bought it yesterday. Today's her birthday. I was planning on dropping it off after our time together." She carefully placed it on Joe's nightstand. Grabbing the purple, red, and white candles, she placed each one above each person. "I can't light it because you're wearing oxygen. Flames and oxygen are not a good combination."

"Still, it's so beautiful," Joe said as his holy thirst ignited once again.

"I couldn't agree more," Dalia replied.

Regaining his composure, Joe continued, "The candelabra is a picture of God. God is a three-person God: Father, Son, and Holy Spirit. They are dancing together in pleasure, in unity and oneness. I don't expect you to understand what I just said, but it's true. It is a mystery. God is one in substance and yet at the same time three persons, Father, Son, and Holy Spirit. See, the thing is, we have offended God deeply. We have all lived shaking an internal fist in God's face. You say you were a runner, that you have run from the reality of eternity. Well, it's God who has placed eternity in your heart. So really, Dalia, you have been running from God, the community at the center of all things."

Dalia swallowed hard and then expressed her inner thoughts. "What you said feels both absolutely beautiful and at the same time terribly tragic. You say the candelabra represents God, three persons in some kind of beautiful dance. Then, at the same time, I have offended God? That doesn't sound good. I don't know what to say. Does the Bible say anything about this? That's where my grandfather would have gone for confirmation."

"Isaiah 53:6 says this: 'All of us, like sheep, have strayed away. We have left God's path to follow our own. Yet the Lord laid on him the sins of us all.'"

"So by running, I have turned my back on God and have lived independently of him, choosing my own way of doing things? That's why I continue to feel so unsettled? It's my soul signaling to me that something is terribly wrong?"

"That's a good way of putting it. Yet, we were never designed to live independently from God. This three-person God is the source of life. When we chose to live independently from God, we actually cut ourselves off from our only source of life. We need air to physically breathe. We need God so our souls can breathe. Without God, our souls suffocate and die."

Dalia's eyes widened again. "So, what are you saying, Joe? Are you saying my soul is dead?"

Joe took a deep breath in and then exhaled. He looked at her with kindness, replying, "Spiritually speaking, that's exactly what I am saying, Dalia. Yet, there's an openness to you that wasn't there before. But don't be deceived. Only God can breathe life into your soul."

Dalia looked at him with confusion. She seemed to be wrestling hard with the words Joe just spoke to her. After a while she summoned the courage to speak. "Those are strong words, Joe. I'm not sure what to do with them right now."

He replied, "The fact that you are wrestling with the words and not dismissing them is a very good sign. You don't need to do anything with them until you are convinced that they are true. God will not force his way into your life. But he will persistently knock at the door of your soul. He's been knocking for quite a while. He's been waiting for you to open the door of your soul so that he may come into you and live inside of you."

They sat in silence for a while.

"Thank you, Joe. I'm going to have to chew on what you have said." She gently took the purple, red, and white candles off the base and placed them all back in her bag.

"Dalia?"

"Yes, Joe?"

"If you could express one thought from our conversation, something that has remained with you, what would it be?"

"One thought." She sat back in her chair, folding her arms. "If this God is real, then he is pretty passionate about making a way for us to know him."

Joe nodded slightly up and down. "That's a great thought to chew on. To be continued, Dalia?"

"Absolutely, to be continued, Joe." She grabbed her bag and headed for the door. When she reached the threshold, she looked back at him. "I can't thank you enough for allowing me to share and for telling me about God, however unsettling at times. It means more than you know."

"It's my pleasure, Dalia. I hope your friend likes the candelabra."

"I hope so too. It has way more meaning now than ever before." With that, she left the room.

Joe closed his eyes for a moment. *Dear Lord, use whatever you can from our conversation to open Dalia's heart to you. I hope I honored you well.*

His whole body jolted when he opened his eyes. He found himself standing in the hallway of a building. Fluorescent lights lit up the corridor, which allowed him to see his surroundings. He saw rooms on either side of the hallway. He decided to go into one of the rooms, where he saw classroom chairs and desks. Up at the front of the room, he saw a chalkboard that spanned the length of the wall. On a small ledge at the bottom of the chalkboard were different color chalk sticks and several erasers. *Must be some kind of conference center.*

He went back into the hallway and walked to the end of it, where it turned ninety degrees to the right and to the left. He looked down either side and saw lockers that stretched from floor to ceiling. It all looked familiar to Joe. He had been here before. Then it came to him. He grabbed his head with both hands. *I can't believe it! This is my old junior high school!*

EIGHT
PERICHORESIS

The living God is not a solitary God.
The living God is not a lonely God.
The living God is the Trinitarian God.
From all eternity, the living God has existed
in community as Community;
in fellowship as Fellowship;
in relationship as Relationship
... And here is the incredibly good, good news.
We human beings were brought into being
to participate with God in that us-ness.
- Darrell Johnson, Experiencing the Trinity

Joe stood there in disbelief. *I haven't seen my junior high school in over sixty years!* He walked to the right, down the corridor until he came to a particular row of lockers. *I'm pretty sure my locker was in this general area. How crazy is this!*

"So, how does it feel being here again?" came a voice directly behind him.

Joe turned around to look but saw no one. By the tone, he could tell it was a woman's voice. A familiar woman's voice. He decided to play along.

"It might be easier to answer your question if you made yourself visible."

"I suppose you're right. But that would take away all the fun," came the voice again while Joe spun around to scan his six o'clock, still seeing no one.

"We used to play hide and seek in these hallways. Remember, JT? Back when we went to school here."

JT? There aren't many people who have called me by that nickname. Joe replied, "Well, whoever you are, you're pretty good at hiding. Are we going to do this until I find you? If so, it may be a while. You're way too good at this game!"

"Truer words have never been spoken," the voice retorted, goading him on.

"Oh, I see. You're a comedian!" replied Joe, joining along in the banter.

Immediately, he heard a jovial laugh coming from his three o'clock from an adjacent hallway. Stealthily, he made his way over to the corner and swiftly looked around it. No one there.

"Are you going to answer my question, JT?" Now the voice seemed to be coming from his nine o'clock. It was a lilting voice full of playfulness and a sense of adventure.

"Oh, you mean about being here again? Yes. Well, I'm finding it hard to fathom, if you must know the truth. But I like being here. It's bringing back some good memories I had long since forgotten."

"I'm so glad, my friend," replied the voice softly.

"Oh, we're friends, are we?"

There was a long silence. Then the voice spoke with a great tenderness. "We are indeed, Joseph Tropea. We are indeed."

Then suddenly he felt a tap on his shoulder. Joseph turned around, and there she was standing before him, violating his personal space. He was startled and stepped backwards, falling to the floor.

He stood up and looked at her. She was wearing an untucked, long sleeve, button down shirt with a delicate red-rose floral pattern and a pair of blue jeans. Her freckled skin was radiant, while her curly auburn hair cascaded down to the middle of her back.

A stunning human being, to say the least. But who is she? He stood there wondering but not saying a word.

"It's good to see you again, JT. It's been a long time."

In that moment, she smiled at him in a certain way that immediately jogged his memory. Joe remembered who she was.

"Carissa?" Joe said with some astonishment.

"Yes, JT. It's me."

He was mystified, "It's been so long. How good it is to see you again!"

"It's good to see you as well. Been a long time. Hey, do you remember how we used to banter near our lockers. I loved making you laugh," she said.

"That was a huge gift to me. I was a pretty intense little kid. I can't tell you how much you lightened my spirit. You helped me take myself a little less seriously. That is until things suddenly changed." Instinctively, he lowered his head.

Looking up ever so slightly, he could tell Carissa was searching to connect with his eyes.

"I'm right here, JT. In the flesh!" She twirled around as she said these words.

"I still can hardly believe it's you. When was the last time we saw each other? I think we were sixteen. Weren't we just starting high school?"

"It couldn't have been any later than that because the car accident happened just shortly after I got my driver's license."

His body stiffened. Falling silent, he slightly lowered his head again.

"JT." She placed her right hand gently on his chin, lifting his eyes to meet her gaze. "I'm right here. I'm doing just fine now. You see?"

Joe could indeed see her standing before him. He stood there speechless, looking at her, this dear sister in Christ standing before him, alive and well, vibrant and happy.

"When I heard about your car accident, I was completely undone. The way it happened, a head-on collision with an eighteen-wheeler, it shook me to the core, Carissa, it really did."

"If it is any comfort to you, it happened so quickly I barely even knew what transpired. Much like how you appeared in our school, I found myself in heaven. It was a great surprise to me, and I will add that when I realized I was in heaven, I wasn't disappointed. On the contrary, I was elated. It was hardest for those left behind, my mother, father, and sister being among many others. But while I was aware of their loss, I experienced none myself. You see, in heaven, everything is complete. I became whole in a way I never experienced on earth. It is hard to explain what it is like to live without the sorrow of suffering . . . not to mention the sorrow of sin. It is something you will just have to experience for yourself, when your time comes to join me in the place where life truly begins."

"Where life truly begins." He repeated the words as if saying them out loud might deepen their impression on him and hasten its coming. Joe believed what she was saying, but nevertheless, doubts rose inside of him.

He decided to speak honestly. "You say those words, Carissa, and I believe you. I really do. But I also struggle to believe. Like that guy in the Bible who said to Jesus, 'Lord, I believe, help my unbelief.' I feel like him. I feel a certain . . . how can I put it . . . a certain contradiction going on inside of me."

Carissa took his arm as they began to walk down the hallway toward the library. She tapped her forefinger on her chin as if seriously pondering his words. Then she replied, "Well, at least you're a walking contradiction, JT." She grabbed his arm tightly and smiled.

He looked down at his legs as he strolled along. Then he looked back at Carissa. "I guess you have a point," Joe replied. Then they broke out in laughter, a banter which felt so familiar to him.

"How I have missed your smile. I know I made you laugh, but you knew how to make me laugh as well. Laughter takes on a whole new meaning in heaven. You'll experience it someday. Someday soon." She leaned into him. "The laughter we enjoyed together as teenagers was just a taste, but a very good taste, of what is fully enjoyed by those in heaven, by those who want to laugh with the laughter of God."

As they opened the door to the library, he caught sight of it. The candelabra. It was resting on a small round table near a tall stack of books. Joe felt his holy thirst immediately rise as he gazed upon the three-person candelabra. The colors of each candle, royal purple, crimson red, and the pure white of a dove, seemed more vibrant than ever. The rhythmic dance seemed to take on greater meaning as Joe noticed that the three persons were not only rotating but seemed to be moving toward each other into the center of their circle and then back out, kind of like a square dance. He looked closer, and to his astonishment, they were actually moving *into* each other, as if to dwell together as one in the center and then back out as three again.

As Joe stood there awestruck by this strange turn of events, he imagined the circle of holy love that the candelabra was meant to portray. While his holy thirst was rising, he closed his eyes, taking in a deep breath and then releasing it. Carissa leaned in a bit closer to whisper something in his ear.

"Perichoresis is quite a mystery, isn't it?"

"What did you say?" Joe turned to face her.

"The reality at the center of all things. Perichoresis. The mutual indwelling of the Father, Son, and Spirit," Carissa said as she too gazed at the revolving candelabra. "Perichoresis," she said again, now holding his gaze.

After a long silence, Joe said, "I'm a bit confused. I know I have heard that word before, but I have never paid much attention to its significance. What does it mean?"

"It literally means 'around in a rhythm.' 'Peri' means around. We get our word 'perimeter' from it. 'Choresis' means rhythm, from which we get the word 'choreography.' The Father, the Son, and the Holy Spirit are in a rhythmic dance of relational love. Isn't that beautiful, JT?"

"Yes, it's incredibly beautiful. Although I myself have never been much of a dancer."

"Believe it or not, you've been taking dance lessons ever since that day in Seattle when you came to know Jesus personally. You've been clunky and out of step many times, but you're getting much, much better. Trust me! As for the future, have no fear. You will have all of eternity to learn what it means to more fully join the dance."

He looked at her with curiosity. "Really? Can you say more?"

"Of course! I would love to say more. Perichoresis is not primarily about physical dancing, although that is one of the fringe benefits in heaven. Everyone in heaven has rhythm. You should see your mother dance! Now that's truly something to behold! It's even more amazing to watch her on the ice. Her ice skating takes on an effortless beauty that is hard to describe. It reflects the effortless beauty of the Trinity."

"My mother never learned how to skate," Joe said as he did his best to stretch his mind to capture the image. It warmed his heart to imagine such a thing. "She always wanted to learn," he added in a mystified timbre.

"You'll get to watch her someday real soon, JT," Carissa replied with a gleam in her eye. "*Real soon*, my friend." Her eyes were welling up with tears. "But keep in mind, there is also a deeper relational meaning to Perichoresis."

"Oh, I would love to hear more about the relational meaning. Can you elaborate?"

"Of course! Questions are always welcomed! Isn't that what you used to say to your philosophy students? At least that's what I was told."

He looked at her inquisitively.

"Your mother chatted with me about it. She never misses an opportunity to brag about you."

It warmed Joe's heart to hear those words. "Thanks for sharing that with me. She's right. Questions are always welcomed. You got me there, Carissa. I can't argue with that. Nor do I want to."

"Then let me answer your wonderful question. Like I said before, Perichoresis speaks to the mutual indwelling of the Trinity."

"Okay, keep going," Joe said as his intrigue grew.

"The Father dwells within the Son. The Son dwells within the Father. The Holy Spirit is the shared love between the Father and the Son, who passes between them, moves in them, through them, then proceeds out from them, into you and me. He is the one who brings us into fellowship with the Father and the Son. Mutual indwelling."

"Now that I think about it, I remember Jesus saying that he is in the Father and the Father is in him. I believe that's in John chapter 14. Is that what you mean by mutual indwelling?"

"Yes. That's part of it. One of your sages used to call it 'reciprocal interpenetration.' I know it's a fancy theological phrase, but it speaks to what it going on within the Trinity. Now we get to be part of it."

"Isn't that something." His voice trembled some as he was plunged into mystery.

"Yes, it is, my friend," she said as she sat down in a chair near the candelabra.

Joe plopped himself down on the ground beside her. Together they watched the candelabra for a while, rotating, then moving into the center, creating one bright colorful flame, then back out again to purple, red, and white.

She spoke again. "They are one God and three distinct

persons. The three do not give up any part of their own personhood by being one in essence."

"It's beyond what I can comprehend."

"You're not alone. It is beyond everyone's comprehension. Mine too. Isn't it amazing that the most basic and foundational truth about God plunges us into mystery? If we want to know God better, we'll have to learn to embrace mystery."

"Honestly, I struggle with that. At times, I feel the pull to figure life out rather than seeing it as a mystery."

"Another one of your sages said that we all feel the pull to live as chess players rather than poets."

Joe furrowed his brow. "What does that mean?"

"It's meant to be a metaphor, not taken literally. Chess players try to figure out life. They plan and strategize, especially when things go wrong. They try their hardest to make life work. Poets, on the other hand, attempt to enter into the mystery of life. When something goes wrong, a poet does not try to figure things out, does not strategize to make life work. Rather, a poet seeks to know God and join the mystery of his purposes when life is not working."

"Oh, that actually sounds inviting," he said as he sat up, pulling his knees to his chest and wrapping his arms around them.

"Can you say more, JT?"

"It seems to be an invitation to stop living out of pressure."

"Yes, the pressure that comes from trying to make life work. 'Come to me all you who are heavy laden, and I will give you rest.' It brings more context to what Jesus was inviting us into. It is an invitation to relax into the mystery that is God: Father, Son, and Holy Spirit."

Joe looked at Carissa sitting there looking at the candelabra. She seemed to be complete in a way that he was not. Her words seemed to be birthed out of a deep joy rising from inside of her, a joy that took pleasure in being able to reveal something unique about the character of God.

He recalled a couple of his trusted friends who loved to talk about the unique Trinitarian signature indelibly placed upon each redeemed soul. Seeing her joy, he wondered about his own soul signature, how he uniquely revealed the character of God. It was an astonishing thought to ponder. He closed his eyes as his holy thirst rose within him.

"Watcha thinkin' JT?" She broke the silence.

"Oh, so many things." He replied.

She smiled and said, "Can you be more specific?"

"Sure. Let me see. Oh, yes. When I was with John Owen earlier . . . do you know John Owen?"

"What a good man!"

"Yes. I experienced him that way too. Anyway, he said that the words that distinguish the Trinity are love, grace, and fellowship. Would you add anything to what he said?"

"I would need to quote another one of your sages. The Father is lover. The Son is the beloved. The Holy Spirit is love itself."

"So, the Father loves the Son. The Son is the beloved of the Father. The Holy Spirit is the love between them? Something like that?"

"Yes. Now that we have the Holy Spirit living in us, we are participants within Trinitarian love. As the apostle Peter said, 'We are partakers in the divine nature.'"

Then Joe's scratched his head. "Some would say that makes us part of God. I recall several people taking this certain view. But it never rang true to me."

"You're right to follow that nudge in you, JT. No, we are not part of the Divine. God is God. He is Creator. We are the created. He is completely other than us. He has existed from eternity past. We had a beginning. He is the source of life because he is life. We are the recipients of his life. We live because he lives. The apostle Peter did say that those who know Jesus personally are now partakers of the divine nature. But that doesn't mean we share in his divinity."

Pressing the point for his own understanding, Joe continued, "That resonates with me. But, again, it could be misunderstood by some to say that we are all part of the divine."

"I suppose it does. In fact, all truths come close to sounding like heresy. Perhaps that is part of the reason why the temptation to go astray is so great. The best way I can explain it is that there are two kinds of glory. God said in the Old Testament that he is God and he cannot share his glory with another. Here, he is talking about his very nature as God. It is impossible for him to share his God-ness with us. When I say 'he,' I also mean all three. The essence of who God is, his deepest state of being, is only shared within the Godhead. In that sense, it can be shared and has always been shared. But since the Father, the Son, and the Holy Spirit are all one God, their deepest state of being, God's *ontology*, is contained within their circle of holy love. Some theologians call this the incommunicable glory of God." She paused and then said, "Are you with me so far?" She grabbed a book off the table and tossed it to him.

Joe caught it with both hands just before it hit his face.

"Nice catch," she said as she let out a laugh.

"What was that about?" he said with surprise.

"Just wanted to make sure you were still awake."

They laughed together.

"Now back to what we were talking about," Carissa said.

"Oh yes, I'm tracking with you, and thanks for taking your time. It feels important."

"It is important. Believing that we are somehow part of God feeds right into our sinful passions. It gives us the illusion of control. It encourages us to take the center when it is God only who is trustworthy and deserving of center stage. Even more than that, it creates pressure, putting us in charge of our own lives, our own change when it is really God who is in charge."

"I can see how that might feed right into my own foolishness as well. I hear you, at least I think I do, in the sense of what it doesn't mean. I'm assuming that you're now going to tell me what it does mean? Being partakers of the divine nature? Am I still tracking?"

"Yes, you are. I love your sense of curiosity. It's one thing to read the Bible. It's quite another thing to understand its relational implications. So, let me continue. We know we cannot share in God's incommunicable glory. However, there is another kind of glory, his communicable glory, that we can share. It is his capacity to love. That is why Jesus tells us, in John 17, that the glory given to him by his Father is now given to us. We are not God nor any part of God, but we do have God's life residing within us. We have the same capacity to love as Jesus loves, because we share the same Spirit, the Holy Spirit. In this sense, we are partakers of the divine nature. God is love and has loved us through the giving of his Son, Jesus. We are able to love because he loved us first."

"So then the glory available to us is the glory of revealing Jesus to other people. That's what you meant by a deeper relational meaning? We can join in perichoresis? We can join the eternal dance? That's why Jesus lived and died, so that we join their dance of Trinitarian love."

"It is one of God's greatest miracles, JT. However, it's important to remember that the love of God is shaped less like a rose-tinted heart and more like a blood-stained cross. The love of God is, by very nature, sacrificial. God gives to fallen humanity all that he has for our good at the greatest expense to himself. Make no mistake, learning to love like Jesus is costly, but it is worth it."

They looked at the three-person candelabra only to notice that the red candle was especially bright. As they sat there gazing at the red candle, Joe was reminded of the cost that was paid for him and for all those seeking to join perichoresis, the divine dance. Simultaneously, they whispered the words, "Thank you, Jesus." Joe instinctively glanced over to look at Carissa, but she was gone.

Joe quickly got up off the floor and looked around for her. "Carissa? Carissa!" he called out. Joe ran out into the hallway. All of a sudden, he heard thunder. He looked up. The ceiling was no longer there. Above him were dark and foreboding clouds. He looked around. Joe was no longer in his junior high school. He was now in the middle of a dark and dense forest. He could see the sun setting in front of him. With his heart pounding, Joe ran toward the setting sun, terrified that he might be left in complete darkness.

"Stop running, Joseph, and turn around," came a calm and resounding voice.

"Nonna, is that you?"

"Yes, it's me, Joseph. Now please stop and do as I say."

"That makes no sense! I can't do it!"

"Yes, you can. Trust me. Trust my heart for you."

"I can't! The sun is setting! It will be completely dark soon! I will be lost forever!"

"Joseph, please listen to me," she said tenderly. "Stop and turn around. Face the darkness. Run into it. The sun will come up on the other side."

Joe listened to her. He turned around and ran into the darkness. He ran for a long time, running around trees and pushing branches out of his way. Then suddenly—*Light! Light! I can see the Light!* The warmth of the sun enveloped his body. He stopped and closed his eyes to take it in. When he opened them again, Joe was in his hospital bed at Bright Star nursing home, awash in the morning sunlight shining through the bay window. *I never thought I'd say this, but it's good to be back in my hospital bed.*

NINE
GETTING YOUR OWN WAY

*There are only two kinds of people in the end: those who say to
God, "Thy will be done," and those to whom God
says, in the end, "Thy will be done."*
- C. S. Lewis, The Great Divorce

Time lingered on and Joe was sleeping a lot more. He
was also eating less. His body could not process food
as it once did.

It was Thursday morning when Dalia walked in. "Oh,
you're awake. How are you doing this morning, Joe?"

"Well, I'm hangin' in there."

"Did you have another one of those mysterious
encounters?"

"As a matter of fact I did, with an old friend of mine who
died back when I was in high school."

"Oh, my goodness. What was that like?"

"It's hard to put into words. I lost part of myself when

she died. I stopped laughing for a long time. To see her again, it was so good. By the way, thanks for the curious question, Dalia. It means a great deal."

"I've learned from the best." She smiled at him.

"So, how have you been lately?" he asked.

"Well, this guy I know has left me with a lot to think about. I'm not sure you know him. His name is Joseph Tropea?"

He laughed. "Yep. I think I've heard of that guy. He's got some good thoughts, but he has a long way to go, mind you."

"Fair enough."

They laughed together.

"Are you up for a shower today?"

"Honestly, I don't think so. The thought of it makes me tired. Can we hold off until this coming Tuesday when you are here again?"

"Sure. No problem at all."

"Thanks," he said as she placed her large bag on the floor. Out of it, she pulled the three-person candelabra and placed it on the table near Maria's picture.

His eyes widened. "I thought you gave that to your friend on her birthday last week?"

"I bought another one. Seeing that you liked it so much, I thought I'd let you keep it for a while. Is that OK with you?"

"Is the pope Catholic? Yes. I'd love that. Are you sure?"

"Of course!" She inserted the purple, red, and white candles over each person. "I can't light it because . . ."

"The oxygen, yes, I know. Not a problem. I'm looking forward to heaven but definitely don't want to go up in a ball of flames."

"I don't want that for you either."

They chuckled some.

"That's so kind of you to bring the candelabra." His holy thirst began to stir.

"My pleasure, my friend. How are you feeling overall?"

"Well my body hurts, like a dull ache everywhere. I'm not eating as much as I used to. So, I'm definitely declining some. It's hard. I don't like seeing myself this way."

She looked at him with moist eyes. "How about I give you a bit of a massage? Just a light one. I can start from your neck and work my way down."

"Really? That would be nice. I don't know what's happening to my muscles. I guess they're atrophying. When the muscle cramps hit, well, it's pretty brutal."

She pulled out some warming oil and stood at the head of his bed and began to lightly massage his neck. "Is that pressure OK?"

"Yes. That's so good. Thank you."

"The warming oil will take some time to take effect, but it should help your muscles relax."

"Okay. I appreciate it."

"You bet. My pleasure."

Some silence ensued as she gently rubbed his neck.

"Do you think I can ask you some questions while I give you a massage? Just some questions that have been lingering. Do you mind? Are you up for it?"

"Absolutely, I've been longing to hear where you went with our last conversation. I know it was a lot to chew on. But first, how do you come into this time? What's going on in you right now?"

"I knew you were going to ask me that."

"It's all right if you don't want to share."

"No, I really want to. It helps me get in touch with my inside self."

"So true. Not many people think about their inside self, in the radical present.

"The radical present?"

"Oh yes, it's something that I learned from one of the people I met. The radical present is where you are in this very moment. Not the previous moment and not the future moment."

"Huh, OK. That makes sense. Well, let me think." She took a few moments in silence. "I feel as though I am more aware of the holy thirst you were talking about the last time we were together. It still amazes me that I have a holy thirst. Very new concept and very hopeful. Yet, I also feel like I need more understanding on some other things."

"I can buy that. So, just to make sure, you are coming in hopeful yet questioning?"

"Yes, in so many words," she said.

A silence ensued.

"What about you, Joe? Where are you in the radical present?"

"Ah, touché, Dalia. I appreciate the question. Now I need to think. Yes, yes, think. Well, I actually feel a lightness in my soul that I haven't felt in a while. Perhaps, because I saw my good friend from years gone by. Yet, even more, I think seeing you and conversing with you . . . it's really a delight to me."

"Thanks, that means a lot." Dalia moved from massaging his neck to massaging his shoulders. "I'm just going to put my hands on your shoulders under your shirt to get some warming oil on them. OK?"

"Yes, thanks."

She gently rubbed his shoulders in a circular motion. "I

think I would like to talk a little more about the problem of sin."

"Wow, nothing like jumping right into the deep end, my friend. Let's do it. What's on your mind?"

"Well, you seem to talk about sin as a relational problem, a shaking of the fist in God's face. I guess it makes sense. If I am honest, I think I have been shaking my fist in God's face for a long time. I just kept myself so busy I was never aware of it. But since I have been talking to you about my life, and the sense of dread I have carried, I've become more cognizant. I guess my question is, how deep is this problem? Is it really so bad? Why couldn't Jesus just come and talk to us about it? You know, reason with us? Did it really need the death of God on the cross?"

"Such good questions. All of them. You've obviously been doing some hard thinking."

"I think I have."

"I'm glad." He looked back and smiled at her. "Let me start by saying yes, sin is a very deep, relational problem. One of the books in the Old Testament, the book of Proverbs, says that foolishness is bound up in the heart of a child. Believe it or not, the sin problem is something that was in us the moment we were conceived."

"Seriously?"

"Seriously. It is not a problem that can be eradicated just by changing our behavior. There is no reasoning with sin. It would be like putting lipstick on a pig. No matter how much makeup you use, a pig is still a pig. We can't make our sin pretty. We can't socialize the sinful energy within us. Although, many people try."

"I think I have been one of those people."

"So have I. In fact, it's still a temptation in me. So, you're in good company, Dalia."

She put some warming oil in her hand and rubbed her palms together. She started massaging his right arm. "That's a relief. I'm glad I'm not alone in this."

"Sin is a universal problem. Every human who has ever lived has been conceived in this condition, everyone except for Jesus."

"Amazing. I mean he's amazing."

He smiled again at her and then looked serious. "Sin is like having stage four cancer of the heart. Reasoning with sin doesn't get us anywhere. Spiritually speaking, we need a heart transplant. Jesus made that possible by dying on the cross."

She applied a little more warming oil to her hands and continued massaging his right forearm. "How's this pressure on your forearm? Still OK?"

"It feels great, thanks so much."

She tilted her head. "So we couldn't do anything about it. Therefore, God did something?"

"You're catching on."

She was pensive for a few moments. "Is there one sin that is worse than all other sins?"

"Another great question. Yes, there is. The worst sin is denying there is a sin problem at all."

"Hmm," she said. "I guess that would make sense. If someone does not believe there is a problem, then they'll never look for the solution."

"It's a great blindness, Dalia. We all come into the world with this blindness. Only God can bring the spiritual healing we need to deal with sin. It's the person of the Holy Spirit who works to open our eyes. That's why the lifelong rejection of the Holy Spirit is the only unforgivable sin. If we reject the Holy Spirit, we refuse to open our spiritual eyes. By rejecting him, we also reject the Father and the Son who gave us the Holy Spirit. I'm not talking about a one-time rejection. If that were the case, none of us would know God. I mean a lifelong rejection. The Trinity keeps the invitation to life open until final breath."

"I guess that's a good thing. I know some people who might be as stubborn as me . . . and that's saying a lot because I'm the most stubborn person I know!"

"I could say the same thing about myself," he was quick to add.

"Joe," she said somewhat tentatively as she moved around the bed to massage his left arm, "what happens to people who reject God permanently, lifelong rejection, as you say?"

He tried to answer as gently as possible. "Dalia, what I am about to tell you is often deeply misunderstood. Yet, when it is understood well it can be lifegiving. I will explain it as best as I can. I want you to listen all the way to the end without jumping to conclusions too quickly. Do you think you can do that?"

"Well, yes. I think so. I trust you Joe."

"Okay then. If a person rejects the fellowship of the Holy Spirit, they also reject the grace of Jesus and therefore cannot experience the tender love of the Father. All that is left is to experience God's wrath in hell for all eternity."

She squeezed Joe's left arm tightly.

Joe winced as his eyes closed. Then he took in a sharp breath.

"Oh, sorry, Joe. I didn't mean to do that. Just reacting to what you just said."

"Ah, it's OK. God's wrath is not a very popular topic these days. Neither is hell. If I could do away with them, I would. It's just not possible. Before I continue, can you say more about your reaction if you can?"

"I'm not sure what to say." She stopped massaging his arm and sat down in a chair beside him.

"Take your time. No rush," he added.

"Well, I guess I need to know . . . actually I want to know more about God's wrath. What exactly is it?"

He smiled at her. "Think about it this way: Trinitarian love is fierce. While God's wrath does not reflect his deepest heart, the love of God cannot be understood without the wrath of God. His wrath is actually part of his love. Divine wrath has nothing to do with God losing his temper when we disobey. It is part of God's being. It is his settled opposition to all that is incongruous with his fierce love and holiness."

She looked at him. "Holiness?"

"Basically, it means that God's relational love is so pure he is set apart from all others. All other loves wither and pale in comparison to God's relationally holy love."

She pondered his words as she walked to the other side of the bed to massage his right leg.

"Are you with me?"

"I think so."

"Can I continue?"

"Please do. How's that pressure on your leg?"

"Great. This is a real gift. Are you able to concentrate on what I'm saying while you're giving me this great massage?"

"Oh yes, I've always been a good multitasker." They laughed as they looked at each other.

"OK, I'll continue. To put what I'm saying another way, God stands against all evil. We all start out evil."

"Seriously? I thought evil was just for the real bad people."

"We can see it easily in tyrannical dictators. We have a hard time seeing it in us. Like I said, it's a real blindness. To go a little further, some think that evil is simply the absence of good. That's not true. Evil has a very real presence. It is deliberate and intentional. It carries a very real energy that people embrace in order to distort, deny, or destroy anything or anyone having to do with God." He looked at her to measure her response. "Are you with me still?"

"I'm tracking, but this is still all so new to me." She walked back to the other side of the bed to massage his left leg.

"Can I continue?"

"Please."

"The people at the foot of the cross were mocking Jesus while he hung there. Evil is personified, in those who reject him, and in the devil who influences those who reject him. Like I said, we are all evil when we come into this world. It's a hard saying. But it's true, and recognizing it can lead to life."

Dalia kept quiet for a while. Then she said, "I'm listening, Joe. If you have more to say, you can keep going."

"Then I will . . . and this is important . . . the wrath of God is not only the wrath of the Father but also the wrath the Son, and the wrath of Holy Spirit. They are one in substance and therefore share in their eternal, white-hot anger toward sin."

"Oh, so it's not just one of them standing against evil. It's all of them?"

"Yes. That's right."

She stopped massaging him and sat for a moment and

closed her eyes. "So what is God's wrath like? How do people experience it?"

Joe thought about it for a moment. "Have you ever experienced anguish during times when you were alone?"

She thought for a moment. "Yes, I have. Actually, I experienced anguish when I left Professor Chesil's office that day I went to see him."

"I've felt it too, in Seattle on that Christmas Eve before I came to know Jesus."

"So then, what are you saying?"

"Those experiences of anguish were a very small taste of God's wrath. Wrath is not so much what God does to us. It is what we do to ourselves. God's wrath is primarily expressed in letting people have their own way. So, God's wrath is not so much imposed by him but rather chosen by people who do not want to be in relationship with him."

"So, people actually choose God's wrath?"

"People choose isolation from God. To be isolated from God is to be isolated from everyone and everything. Wrath is the only thing we can experience in our unforgiven, isolated, sinful state."

She kept her eyes closed, slightly nodding her head up and down. "Is there more?"

"Yes, those who diminish God's wrath also miss the sheer beauty and radically other-centered love displayed on the cross. The Father, Son, and Holy Spirit knew that no one could pay the price of sin without paying the price of eternal isolation. So, they devised a way to take care of sin by enduring their own wrath within the community of their fierce love. The only way for people to join in the eternal dance was for the triune God to absorb the punishment of eternal isolation within the circle of their love. Jesus endured this God-shared wrath that was meant for us."

"That's sounds like good news," Dalia said in a quivering voice.

"It is good news for those who can accept it. God never violates free will. Either we let God endure his own wrath within their community of radical love or we endure it for eternity."

She opened her eyes and looked at him. "Do you have more to say about wrath?"

"Just one more thing."

"OK. I'm listening." She went to the foot of the bed. Pouring some warming oil in her hands, she began massaging his right foot.

"People who reject or diminish the reality of God's wrath do not understand the relational implications of their decision. By doing so, they undermine the fierce nature of God's love. Therefore, love is diminished in all their relationships into sentimentality, or mere empathy. There is no strength or solidness to their love. Consequently, no one can find true rest in them. They are not solid enough to love others fiercely. In the name of love, they excuse relational violations, in others and in themselves, that need to be brought out into the light for the sake of the one guilty of those relational violations."

She stopped massaging his foot for a moment and looked at him. "I'll be honest. There is part of me that fights against what you are saying and another part which resonates with it."

"That's probably a good sign."

"Really?" She tilted her head as she took in his words.

"Yes. I would not expect you to just swallow all this

without really thinking about it first. Your heart must come to terms with what I'm saying. You have the freedom to believe it or to not believe it."

"I appreciate that," she said as she applied warming oil to her hand and began to massage his left foot.

"Keep wrestling with it. Ask the Holy Spirit to open your spiritual eyes."

"All right, I will."

Some silence ensued.

"Joe?"

"Yes, Dalia?"

"You mentioned hell earlier. Can you put a few more words to what that means?"

"Sure. I'll give you a couple of thoughts, the first one I read from a Russian novelist. Among many other things, hell is the inability to love or be loved."

"Huh, OK," She said. "What's the second thought?"

"Hell is also an eternally fixed state."

"Oh. Wow," She said in a somewhat shocked manner.

"So then, hell is the eternally fixed inability to love or be loved."

Dalia seemed to brood over those words for a good while. Then, connecting the relational dots, she exclaimed, "Does that mean that heaven is the eternally fixed *ability* to love and to be loved?"

Joe replied, "That's right."

He closed his eyes and took a deep breath, then, letting it out, said, "These are weighty matters, I know."

After a long silence, Dalia replied, "But if they weren't weighty, I guess they wouldn't mean much?"

"Better to have weighty words that disrupt us than flimsy

words that assuage that which is foolish in us. True love disrupts, but for very good reasons," he added.

"Can I ask one more question?"

"Sure."

"In light of all this, what do I need? How does this all relate to my life?"

"I'm glad you went there. Let's talk about it. Think about how troubled you have felt over the years. You have not been able to shake it because something is wrong. Something is wrong between you and God. Because of your choice of independence, your sins have eternally separated you from God. There is nothing you can do about it. So, God did something. God took care of the price for your sins, the punishment for your sins, and absorbed them into his own circle of love. The Father gave his Son over to death, the Son willingly died, and the Holy Spirit was moving powerfully in Jesus while he was dying on the cross. Keep in mind also that while Jesus was dying on the cross, there was a separation that occurred between the Father and Son that had never occurred in all eternity past."

"Wow, that's hard to wrap my mind around. They had never been separated before until Jesus bore our sins on the cross? If that's true, then I'm astounded."

"You and me both. You see, Dalia, they were all involved in different ways. The Father gave. The Son bore. The Spirit moved. They were all involved in order to get you to the dance, the eternal dance of the Trinity."

She closed her eyes again. "So, I need . . ."

"Right now, only one thing, Dalia. God's forgiveness. That's all you need. Only Jesus can give that to you. You remember your vision of the lion crouching in the tall grass? Jesus is the lion. But he is not waiting to destroy you. On the contrary, he is waiting to forgive you. You see, Dalia, the lion is also the lamb. That's the picture of Jesus on the cross. The lamb was slaughtered so our sins might be forgiven."

"That's a disturbing picture. But I guess the cross was a disturbing way to die."

"There's no getting around that, Dalia. Our sin problem runs very deep. Only this kind of death, by the Son of God, could effectively deal with the problem. On the cross, Jesus won a great victory, the greatest victory of all! And then, three days later, he came back to life. The resurrection! The cross is the victory. The resurrection is the celebration of the victory. Since he rose from the dead, we can too with him, and in him. We can join the eternal dance."

There was an awkward pause between them.

Joe, sensing it, said, "Are you with me, Dalia? Or have I said too much? Do you need clarification?

"No, no. I'm good," she said as she took in a deep breath.

"It's a lot to ponder, I know," Joe said with some resignation.

"But if it's true, then it's important to know. Yes?" she said to him.

"Yes," he replied.

They sat in silence for a long while. She put her things back in her bag quietly and then turned to Joe and said, "Well, that was a lot to say. You must be very tired, my friend. Thank you for sharing with me. You've given me a lot to think about. Now, how about you get some rest." She touched his arm gently in a gesture of appreciation. "Enjoy the candelabra, my friend. I'll leave it with you for now." Then she turned to grab her bag.

"I can't thank you enough for the massage. It has done this withering body of mine a world of good."

"It's my pleasure."

"Is there a thought you will leave with today, Dalia?"

She exhaled. "Oh my, one thought. Well, I guess I have one thought. It's a pretty simple thought."

"Sometimes the simplest thoughts are the most profound."

"You think so?"

"I really do."

They lingered in silence for a moment.

"What's your thought, my friend?"

"My thought is this." She looked at him teary-eyed. "God must really love us to go through all that they did to get us to the eternal dance."

"Yes. Yes. What a good thought. So rich. So good."

With bag in tow, she said, "I'll leave you for now, Joe. Thank you for taking the time to explain these hard concepts to me. I'll be back to see you on Tuesday. Maybe you'll be up for a shower then? I look forward to seeing you soon."

"To be continued, Dalia?"

"Absolutely, to be continued, Joe." Then she left the room.

As Joseph closed his eyes with Dalia on his mind, he felt an eerie feeling overtake him. His room suddenly turned dark, and a blistering wind enveloped him. He blinked his eyes and found himself on the edge of a high cliff overlooking an ominous chasm. A distorted figure approached him, standing on a cliff on the opposite side of the chasm. Although he could not be sure, the figure had some resemblance to a human being. In his young body once more, Joe braced himself and somehow knew this was not going to be a life-giving conversation. He was in for something much, much different.

TEN
THE INABILITY TO LOVE

If you insist on having your own way, you will get it.
Hell is the enjoyment of your own way forever.
- Dorothy Sayers, Dante's Purgatory (Intro)

As Joe's eyes adjusted to the foreboding scene, it seemed apparent that he was meant to have an encounter with this distorted figure. However, they were too far away from each other, and there was no way of getting across the chasm that separated them. That was until the figure pointed anxiously, with a gnarled finger, to a pair of peninsulas on either side of the chasm, a place where both cliffs came dangerously close to touching each other. Both Joe and the figure walked to their respective peninsulas and were now standing only a few feet apart. Either one of them could now easily step over the abyss, which was reduced to the width of only one stride. Neither of them moved.

Sensing a warm light behind him, Joe turned around to

see a crystal-blue sky speckled with pure white clouds. There were mountain peaks in the far distance, and some of them were snowcapped. Blanketing the ground in front of the mountains were lush greens fields. There were also large square patches of wheat stalks protruding up toward the sky, which almost seemed thoughtfully placed within the fields. He looked to the left and to the right, astonished that the mountain peaks stretched in both directions as far as the eye could see. It was a beautiful sight to behold. He looked down and noticed that he was barefoot, standing on green grass wet with dew carpeting the ground beneath his feet. He closed his eyes, taking a deep breath in and then out. It felt good. He opened his eyes once again and looked at the mountains, magnificent in appearance. He let his mind wander a little, picturing a walk toward those majestic peaks. He imagined that he might find the City of God in those mountains, like in John Bunyan's *Pilgrim's Progress*. At the thought of this, his heart felt a deep yearning. But Joe intuitively knew that such an adventure was not the purpose of this encounter. Warily now, he turned to face the figure and felt a chill run through his body.

The figure spoke. "Your land is so bright. Who would ever want to live there?"

A person? Or what is left of a person?

He glanced beyond the figure, surveying the landscape behind . . . him. *Is this actually a him?* He thought so but wasn't quite sure. It looked as though the figure was standing on the edge of some sort of fenced-in park, like a prison yard. There was no green grass, no mountains, and no warm light, just a very dim light coming from nowhere in particular, like a light one might experience in a seedy bar. The ground seemed to be made out of some kind of concrete, or asphalt.

He couldn't be sure. Strewn about the square park were what looked like tables. Each table had only one chair. All the chairs were made out of some kind of hard plastic. Both the chairs and the tables appeared bolted to the ground. On some of the tables were plates, bowls, and utensils made out of what appeared to be dull steel. Some of the plates and bowls were scattered upon the hard ground along with utensils, which did not appear to be used.

Joe struggled to understand what all this meant when the figure gave a cough as if clearing its throat.

"Are you going to say something?" said the figure with an edge in its voice.

Joe, a little caught off guard, replied, "Oh, I didn't know you wanted me to respond. How should I address you?"

"What do you mean?" retorted the figure.

"Well, I mean, what is your name?"

"Name?"

"Yes, your name."

There was a long pause.

"I once had a name. I don't really recall. Yet, now, perhaps I do recall a little. I believe it was a man's name. No matter. Such things make no difference in this . . . this *place*," The figure said with a strange mixture of repulsion and fondness.

"Oh." Joe looked at the ground, not knowing what to say in response. Then, mustering up a bit of courage, he asked, "If you don't have a name, how do you distinguish yourself from others? Do the others have names? I'm assuming you're not the only one who lives here. Yes?"

With a slight look of disgust, the figure responded, "There *are* others, of course." The figure said these words as if Joe had asked a stupid question. "But there is no need, nor is there any desire to distinguish ourselves from each other. Why should there be? We don't talk *with* each other here. Yet, sometimes we talk *at* each other. We are always looking to our own selves." Pointing his gnarled finger at what seemed to be his chest with strong emphasis, he said, "I Am that I Am."

"I Am that I Am?" asked Joe tentatively. "That's the phrase God used to describe himself."

"Here, we are gods to ourselves."

Joe, still not understanding, tilted his head slightly.

"We all look after *only* ourselves?" said the figure in the form of a question that was not a question. "We avoid interacting with each other at all costs. That way things don't have to get messy."

"Messy? How would things get messy?"

"You would have to be one of us to really know." Then looking Joe up and down, the figure said, "You are most certainly not one of us."

These words dripped with condescension, and Joe was suddenly aware of feeling quite small. He felt a strong urge to shrink back, to cower under the verbal insults of the figure. His shoulders sagged, and he broke eye contact with the figure, casting his gaze toward the ground.

But Joe knew that while he was only one person, and while perhaps small, he was a person of substance. The life of God resided in the center of his soul. He recalled Jesus on the cross, how incredibly solid he was as people hurled insults at him. He recalled what the book of Hebrews said about Jesus, "who for the joy that was set before him endured the cross, despising the shame." It was the words "despising the shame" that seemed to resonate in the moment.

What would it mean for me to despise the shame right now? Could I love this distorted man with the love of God, here, in the radical present? Could I despise the shame that is being hurled at me by the figure, without despising him? Yes, love the distorted man who stands before me and despise the shame that is pouring out of the distorted man toward me. Yes. Yes, God help me, yes.

As the Holy Spirit whispered this truth to him, instead of shrinking back, Joe lifted his shoulders, standing straight and tall. He looked the figure squarely in his distorted eyes. The figure took a step back and then stepped forward again. The shift in Joe's body language seemed to allow the figure to experience Joe's inner solidness.

As he sensed the life of God pulsating within him, a mixture of emotions rose up in Joe's soul. A profound sense of sadness and compassion overwhelmed him. The shame, while still threatening him, no longer knocked him off his center.

The figure, now sensing this, began to slightly tremble. A quiet indignation grew in him, and his face twisted in distortion even more. As his intensity increased, he railed, "Are you here to condemn me? You are, aren't you! That's why you've come! Well, as you can see, I am already condemned! So, you are wasting your time!"

Joe's eyes were moist with tears as compassion continued to rise in him. In a low whisper, he responded to the figure, "I'm not here to condemn you. It seems you have taken care of that all by yourself." Substance and gentleness mingled inside of Joe as he said these words.

"Then why? Why are you here? To torture me! Yes, you're here to torture me even more! Have I not experienced enough torture? Can't you leave well enough alone?" As the figure spoke, like a man turning into a gargoyle, his distorted body seemed to rise to an intimidating stature.

Joe remained calm, his soul steady and sure. Without raising his voice, he answered, "To be honest with you, I have no idea why I'm here. Perhaps you are meant to teach me something? I'm not sure."

At the sound of these words, the figure seemed to relax a little. A smug and pseudo-satisfied look appeared on his face at the thought of being the instructor as opposed to the instructed.

After a chilling silence, the figure responded, "Well, I'm glad you feel that way. After all, I *do* have things to teach despite living . . . here." His voice trailed off. Then regaining his tenor, he finished his thought. "We all have a need to be needed, don't we?"

Joe couldn't help but ask, "The need to be needed? Wouldn't you consider that an energy that emerges from our own self-centeredness? I have experienced this energy before, but it never seems to come from a clean place within me."

"Self-centeredness is all we have . . . here. There are no other options." The figure looked around.

"Oh really? That's a real shame."

As Joe scrambled to understand this, the figure spoke again. "So, you think I'm worthless then? Because I'm self-centered?" said the figure, trying to twist Joe's words.

"What, no!" Joe was quick to reply. "I would never call you worthless. But, looking at you, another word does come to mind."

"What word is that?" The edge in the figure's voice returned.

Joe waited a while before answering, largely because he

didn't know if it would be a good idea. Not that he was afraid. He wasn't. He was more concerned not to add insult to injury.

The figure seemed to sense that Joe was quietly deliberating whether or not to answer. He impatiently replied, "Go on, you can tell me." This was asked in a polite manner, but it did not feel kind.

After a long, compassionate look into the figure's distorted eyes, Joe decided to tell him, "Tragic. The word I had in mind was tragic." Joe steadied himself for the response.

To his surprise, the figure said, "I wholeheartedly agree. It is tragic. This whole situation is tragic. I am tragic! How I came to deserve being here I do not know. But it is without question very, very tragic." The figure said these words in such a way that did not own any wrongdoing, but as though the tragedy of his situation happened upon him, a basically decent man, by surprise.

"So, you don't believe that you deserve to be here?" inquired Joe.

"No, I don't. I'm basically good, at least good enough. I'm not saying that I haven't done anything wrong. I'm not perfect after all. Who is? I think I'm in pretty good company when I say that I did my best in life and am doing my best in this . . . wherever this is. It is a travesty that no one takes notice. There are many others here who are way worse than me. They have no names, so it would prove difficult to point them out. But believe me, stick around long enough and you will see what I mean. Would you believe that I am sharing this vile place with actual murderers? When I say murderers, I mean mass murderers, almost wiping out entire countries! Now, come on! How is it even plausible that we are living anywhere near each other?" Looking confused, he continued, "I deserve better. Maybe not the best but definitely better than this. You know I used to be an avid churchgoer in my time . . . as best as I can recall. I believed in Jesus Christ. Not in a literal sense, in more of a figurative sense. Yet, I did my best to follow the moral example of those make-believe stories in the Bible. I was a morally decent . . . uh . . . man . . . yes man . . . I think. People looked up to me. Here, in this contemptible place, no one looks up to anyone. Everyone is consumed with looking at themselves."

"So you are waiting for someone to take notice of your goodness?" asked Joe in bewilderment.

"Yes. I feel justified in saying that. After all, one needs to have self-confidence about such things. I used to teach others about self-confidence, thinking well about oneself, getting rid of any negative thoughts about oneself. After all, aren't we all basically good? Even those awful mass murderers, deep down, are probably just badly misunderstood people. They never had the opportunity to believe in their goodness. Bad family dynamics and all, abused and misunderstood."

Joe, speaking out of God-confidence rather than self-confidence, replied, "That's strange, because those who live in freedom, in the beautiful place where I am destined to be, they are all aware of how thoroughly bad they were on earth. None of those in heaven would even dare say that they were basically good people. They would say that they used to be thoroughly bad, tainted in every way by a self-entitled spirit. When you talk about murderers . . . Jesus told us that anyone who flies off the handle toward another is actually a murderer. I, the man you are looking at right now, am a murderer. I have murdered many people with my anger. Not physically, not with my hands, but with the deadly energy in my heart and with my self-entitled words. You could say in a very literal sense that heaven consists of people who are all *forgiven murderers.* I'm afraid if you are waiting for someone to notice your goodness, you'll be waiting for all eternity. There is no one who is good inherently. Not even one. Well, except one."

The figure raised his contorted hand and said in a politely distant tone, "We do not use his name in the literal sense, only in the metaphorical sense."

"Metaphorical?"

"Yes, metaphorical."

"I don't understand." Joe couldn't be sure, but he thought he saw the figure roll his eyes.

"I recently had an argument with a group of . . . of . . ."

"People?" Joe finished his sentence.

"Yes, something like that. Anyway, we were all talking at each other, and it was clear to me immediately that the others, who were clearly in the wrong, needed to have a 'come to Jesus' moment."

"A 'come to Jesus' moment?"

"Precisely. It was a metaphor . . . for trying to help people get along, to help people communicate better."

With a childlike innocence, Joe asked, "But how can there be any real unity without knowing the real Jesus?"

The figure snapped, "Please *do not* use his name that way." He was doing his best to couch his anger in a polite tone.

Joe breathed in sharply . . . and then a silence ensued. Joe's eyes welled up with tears again as his gaze remained on the distorted man.

"You've just committed murder . . . just now . . . do you see?"

"I don't see that at all. I was trying to be polite."

"Yes. Your words did sound polite, but it was the energy behind the words that was murderous."

The figure, now caught in his own lie, snapped back again. "Well, if that's true, then so be it. What is the Greek word for that phrase in the Bible? Amen. How can it be my fault? I am that I am. Therefore, you should accept me as I am. My truth is my own. Your truth is your own. We should accept each other as we are, should we not? All truth is relative after all."

Joe spoke his next words with a great amount of gentleness. "You mean, of course, every truth except the one you just mentioned."

The figure, feeling caught again, could only manage to say, "What?"

"If all truth is relative and if there are no objective truths as you say, then that very statement has to be true for *everyone*. It is, in fact, objective. When you say, 'all truth is relative,' you are actually speaking objectively. So, what you are saying implodes on itself. It cannot be true. It is by itself objective. You see, it is impossible to get away from the fact that there is truth that pertains to everyone. All people are murderers, except for one. That is an objective truth. All people need the forgiveness God offers. That is also an objective truth. I say these things not to chastise you. It is more of a confession. My confession to you. I am a murderer in need of forgiveness, and I have received forgiveness from Jesus Christ."

The figure, clearly shaken but feigning calm, said, "I told you not to use his name in that way. Don't you have any sense of respect for the wishes of others?"

"I truly do want to respect you. If only you could first see it in me, my need for forgiveness, then maybe you could see it for yourself? But if you would rather not hear what I have to say, then I will respect your wishes. I will remain silent." Joe's voice cracked as he said these words, his compassion leaking out of him.

The figure was a bit taken aback and seemed to be disarmed for a moment, surprised by the unforced invitation of Joe's words. Then, doing his best to sound courteous, the figure responded, "We must have a very different understanding when it comes to the meaning of respect. Respect in this place has to do with keeping to yourself, not ruffling any feathers. We tolerate each other here by keeping to ourselves."

"In heaven, and to a great degree on earth, those who are forgiven by God learn to love each other, which means talking to each other in a way that offers life, the very life of God. It can be very disruptive, but it is also life-giving."

"Here, we all have made god in our own image and in our own likeness. It seems to go better for us that way."

Joe, realizing he was getting nowhere, decided to refrain from saying any more. While the figure had dismissed Joe, it was clear to him that the distorted man wanted to keep talking. *He probably hasn't talked with anyone in quite some time.*

The figure monologued for a while, jumping from one conversation to another. Joe was so flustered he turned to leave.

"You were looking behind me before?" said the figure.

"Well, yes, I was," Joe said as he turned back to look at him.

"You were wondering about the tables, among other things?" the figure continued, probing Joe's curiosity.

"Yes."

"Would you like me to tell you?"

"Please do," Joe said, eager to understand the bizarre nature of the scene.

"Every once in a while, the others come here. We all sit at one of the tables, alone. Like I said before, we don't want things to get messy. So, we give each other plenty of space. We gather a plate and a bowl and some utensils. Then we sit and wait."

"Wait for what?"

"We wait for food. You see, we here, in this . . . place, are the eternally starved. There is no such thing as satisfaction here. No satisfaction physically and no satisfaction . . ." Again the figure struggled to find the word.

"Relationally?" inquired Joe.

"Why yes . . . yes . . . yes," said the distorted man forlornly as his voice trailed off.

Joe wondered if he was imagining what a small taste of relational satisfaction might be like.

"We don't even have the satisfaction of killing ourselves. Nevertheless, we wait with half-baked hope that one day we will have one little taste of physical satisfaction. Some morsel of bread. Some refreshment of water."

"But nothing ever comes," Joe said, one step ahead of the figure.

"Correct," said the distorted man in fuming resignation.

The figure continued, "After waiting for a while . . . we don't know how long because there are no clocks here . . . we all get fed up and smash the plates and bowls down upon the ground. But they just bounce off the surface. We don't even have the satisfaction of watching them shatter into pieces. It is as though everything here is in a fixed state. Nothing can change. We try to upend the tables, but they remained fixed to the hard surface. We even try to throw the chairs, but those, too, are fixed to the ground. It's at these moments that brawls tend to break out. There is at least the smallest amount of satisfaction . . . if you can even call it that . . . in causing each other pain. But it never lasts for very long. We are a commune of the eternally unsatisfied. We have nothing to offer each other but pain."

"The eternally fixed inability to love or be loved," Joe replied, recalling the words he said to Dalia.

As the figure did his best to straighten his arched back, he said, "Well . . . yes, but it is not as bad as you might think."

Joe replied, shaking his head in disbelief, "I can't imagine anything worse."

All the figure could manage to do was let out a "Humph."

The two of them remained silent for a while. After Joe took all this in, he asked the figure one final question. "So, if you are so miserable in this place . . . I think we both know that you are in hell . . . why don't you do something about it? You could ask Jesus for forgiveness. Look, right here, you could receive his forgiveness and just step over to my side with one stride. One confession. One step. Then your misery would be over."

"What makes you think I need forgiveness? Even if I did need it, what makes you think I would want it?"

Stunned, Joe said, "You mean you really don't? You would rather starve eternally in hell, unable to love or be loved, than be with Jesus?"

The figure put his gnarled hands over his distorted ears. Trembling with quiet rage, he said in his most politely distant tone, "Yes . . . and I told you before, please do not use his name so literally."

In that moment Joe was reminded that God didn't send people to hell. Those in hell were there of their own choosing. He thought of God, how he respected the free will of all humans. *Didn't C. S. Lewis once call free will "the intolerable compliment"?*

Just then, the sky lit up in colorful flame: purple, red, and white. Joe looked up at the flames in wondrous awe. The figure, however, started to scream. A commotion began to develop behind the figure. Other distorted human beings suddenly poured into the prison yard.

All of them looked anxiously at the plates and the bowls, shielding their distorted eyes from the flames above them. Then, as the figures noticed there was no food, in a feverish frenzy, they started throwing the steel plates and the steel bowls at each other, smashing each other in the face, then jabbing each other with the utensils. There could be heard weeping and gnashing of teeth.

The figure, standing quite close to Joe, instinctively reached out his gnarled hands toward him. The helpless look on his face seemed to communicate a desire to be rescued. Instinctively, Joe extended his arms out toward the figure so he could pull him over the chasm onto his side. Just as their fingers were about to touch, the figure pulled back. Clenching his hands into tight fists, he began to shriek with indignation. Joe lost his balance and began to fall forward. He tried to regain his stability by rotating his arms in a backwards motion. He over calculated. His feet slipped out from under him on the wet grass, and he fell into the chasm.

As he plunged into the darkness, Joe closed his eyes and cried out in horror, "NO! NO! PLEASE NO!" Then he opened his eyes and gasped for air. As he became oriented to his surroundings, all that could be heard was the sound of the clock on the far wall, ticking. He was, once again, in his room at Bright Star nursing home. When Joe realized where he was, he let out a deep sigh of relief. He caught sight of a cross hanging on the wall near the doorway, wondering who put it there. As he gazed at the cross, he thought about the agony Jesus endured to save Joe from himself, from hell, and gratitude swelled in his heart.

ELEVEN
THE WOUNDED SURGEON

In his right hand he held seven stars, from his mouth came a
sharp two-edged sword, and his face was like the
sun shining in full strength.
- Revelation 1:16, ESV

Joe lay quietly in his bed, shuddering slightly at the recollection of his last encounter. While he found it difficult to grasp the fact that such a place as hell actually existed, he marveled over how deeply committed God remained to giving each human being the respect of free will, the freedom to choose him or not to choose him. His mind went back to a time in his life, back before his miraculous conversion in Seattle, when he had no need for God and no desire for God. At least that was what he convinced himself to believe. He quivered at how little difference there was between him and the distorted man he'd recently met.

Back then, my own sin was just as deep, just as destructive to relationships, just as offensive to God. Even now, as a Christian, the inner battle between the presence of sin and the presence of the Holy Spirit continues to wage war. The same deadly energy in that distorted man still exists in me. But that deadly energy does not define who I am. There is a deeper power at work in me. He quivered with joy.

Is it actually possible to believe in Jesus Christ your whole life and not know Jesus Christ? The figure believed in Jesus Christ, at least in some metaphorical sense. Yet, he never received Jesus Christ for who he claimed to be, a real person, the Son of God, God the Son. He closed his eyes while his whole body shuddered.

The only way to know Jesus Christ is to receive him as a real person, as the real living, breathing Savior. Each person, as a someone who eternally exists, has the dangerous privilege of deciding for themselves. No wonder C. S. Lewis called free will the "intolerable compliment." At the thought of this, Joe shook his head in unqualified amazement.

For the next five days, Joe was in and out of consciousness. When he was awake he noticed that he was drinking less. The decrease of food and water caused him to lose weight rapidly.

Dalia walked into the room. She seemed happy to see he was awake. She smiled and waved to him. "Hello, my friend."

His heart warmed at the sight of her, and the weighty thoughts that consumed his mind were somehow lightened, but not completely forgotten, by just one look at her face.

"How do you like the cross I hung up near the doorway?" she said as she gave it a glance over her shoulder.

It was evident to Joe that his voice was weakening. He said with some effort, "You put that there?"

Her eyes widened some. "Your voice seems weaker. Is it harder for you to talk?"

He closed his eyes and nodded. "It is."

There was a pause. Then Dalia replied, "Yes, I put the cross there. Do you want to know where I got it?"

He nodded his head up and down.

"It was my grandfather's. He had it hanging in his room, just like that, right near the doorway. I suppose he placed it there to remind him."

"To remind him of what?" Joe said with no small amount of curiosity.

"Of what truly matters." These words seemed to pour out of Dalia with a quiet power, and they lingered, like sweet perfume, in the space between them.

After a long pause, Joe took a deep breath in and managed to say, "There's something different about you, Dalia."

"I would like to think so, Joe. I did a lot of thinking after our last conversation. Well actually, more than just thinking. I did quite a bit of . . . of . . ."

Joe helped her find the words. "Soul searching?"

"That's close. It's felt more like soul struggling. To be honest with you, I have been quite unsettled since our last two conversations."

Joe waited for her to continue, hanging on every word.

"I was really wrestling with your words, Joe. To a large degree, I'm still wrestling but now in a new way, in a way I've never struggled before."

"I'd be surprised if you weren't, to some extent, unsettled by my words."

She looked at him with confusion and surprise. "Really?" she said, a bit dumbfounded.

"It's like a farmer tilling a field that has become hard and dry. It's got to be stirred up, deeply agitated, before the water can penetrate. In this case, it's life-giving water that is being offered to you. So, your soul, in a very real sense, needs to be plowed up."

"Hmm," Dalia responded. "I guess that does make some sense," she said in a grappling sort of way.

Finding a second wind, he said, "There is more to say about your ongoing struggle. But I don't want to get ahead of you. It sounds like you have more to share. Something important it seems?"

"Something very important." She added, "At least I think so."

"Then go ahead, friend, I'm all ears."

"Thanks," she said genuinely. "Now, where to start . . ."

Joe waited in silence.

"Your words about God's wrath really disturbed me on one level. On another level, they made sense to me. To hear that I had a soul, wow, I had never thought about that before. I thought I was just a cluster of biological components that one day would stop working, then wither into dust. But to come across those words in Ecclesiastes about 'eternity in the human heart' and then to get confirmation from you about having an eternal soul, that touched something deep in me. Then, on top of that, hearing that I had an actual thirst for God, that really blew me away."

She paused at this point to gather her thoughts. Joe remained silent and simply waited for her to speak.

Dalia continued, "But then to hear that my soul was dead. Dead? Really? That was difficult to hear. I think what you meant was that even though I am an eternal soul with a thirst for God, I was unresponsive and unable, by my own effort, to make my soul responsive?"

Joe nodded up and down without saying a word.

"That was hard to hear, but I'm glad you didn't sugarcoat things. I knew there was something wrong. I just didn't know how badly wrong. Even though your words hurt, it was like a healing-hurt, like the blade of a surgeon's scalpel giving me a heart transplant, to use your words."

Joe marveled at the metaphor and thought how true those words were, even for him. He smiled at her, with moist eyes, and said gently, "Go on, friend."

"Well, this put a whole new spin on things. I knew I was a runner, Joe. Like I said, I have been running all my life. But to then hear that my condition was so dire, that I needed some kind of soul surgery to be made alive to God . . . that was an entirely new dimension for me. I really wrestled with it, Joe. I really did."

He instinctively knew that wasn't the end of the story, so he waited with bated breath for what Dalia would say next.

"That's when I came across this strange poem. It was in the back of my grandfather's Bible, written in his handwriting on a back page." She then pulled out the dog-eared Bible and flipped to the back. She then read the words:

> The wounded surgeon plies the steel
> That questions the distempered part;
> Beneath the bleeding hands we feel
> The sharp compassion of the healer's art
> Resolving the enigma of the fever chart.

After a long pause, Joe said incredulously, "T. S. Eliot."

"Yes, I know," Dalia replied.

He gave her a sideways glance. "How?"

She smiled and, shrugging her shoulders, said, "Thank God for the internet."

They both shared in a moment of gentle laughter.

When the mirth subsided, Dalia continued, "That little poem spoke directly to my present experience. Jesus is the wounded surgeon, isn't that right?"

"That's right, Dalia."

"The bleeding hands, that's a reference to his crucifixion?"

"Yes, I believe so."

"He's performing a kind of soul surgery?"

"He's pretty good at that, Dalia."

"And those words 'sharp compassion,' those words are incredibly relevant to me. I am aware of a kind of soul surgery going on in me, but it's hard to put it into words."

Joe kept silent.

She continued, "It seems, with compassion, Jesus is performing this surgery for my good."

"If I could only share with you how many times I've experienced the same thing. Believe me when I say that you are in very good company."

"I appreciate that." But she wasn't finished. "Those last words really drove things home, 'resolving the enigma of the fever chart.' Am I right in saying he is talking about the problem of sin? The fever is our sinful condition, and, like you said, Jesus is the only one that can take care of this problem. Am I in the ballpark?"

"You're definitely in the ballpark. Such timely words for you, huh?"

"Without question."

A quiet moment ensued. Then Dalia said, "I did something I have never done before."

"Yes?" Joe said earnestly.

"I got down on my knees and prayed."

"You did. Oh wow," Joe said with amazement. Even though he had watched this happen with others, it never grew old to hear a person opening their heart to God for the first time. His curiosity getting the best of him again, he asked, "What did you pray for, Dalia?"

She took a moment to gather her rising emotions. Choking back the tears, she replied, "I said, 'Jesus, please do the healing surgery in me that only you can do. Open my heart so that I may *want to want* you. I have no power to do this on my own. Thank you, Lord, for forgiving my sins. I believe you, and I receive you . . . as best as I know how.'"

After a while, Joe responded with quiet delight, "That's a beautiful prayer."

She responded tenderly, "Thank you, for more than you can imagine."

Deflecting the compliment a little, Joe replied, "Well, it's like you said, Dalia. I am just the messenger. All the rest was the Father, Son, and Holy Spirit working in your soul. The praise and glory are reserved for the holy three-in-one."

"That sounds magnificent," she concurred.

"If only we could see the holy throng of angels and saints around the throne, we would be overwhelmed by the celebration and the singing."

She smiled, and a hush came over them. "Are you still good to talk, Joe? I can tell you are exerting a lot of energy to talk."

"I'm good. I'll let you know if I need to stop. Thanks for

asking." Shifting the conversational gears a bit, Joe asked, "Dalia, you mentioned that you were now struggling in an entirely new way. Would you like to put more words to that? I'm eager to listen."

Still thinking about his physical state, she said, "Yes, I would. But first, let's get you showered. Are you up for it, Joe? It will do you some good."

He replied with some reticence, "OK, let's do it."

She proceeded to shower him in the usual gentle manner, communicating with him to make sure none of her sudden movements were causing him pain. She made sure to proceed slowly, and when she finally finished, Dalia gently helped Joe get back into his bed. When she had him situated, she pulled out some hand lotion. She squeezed out a measured portion and, little by little, began to massage Joe's hands, one at a time. While Joe could barely move his arms, he could still enjoy the sensation of touch. His body relaxed into the simple gift that was being given, and he was reminded once more that some of the simplest gifts in life end up being the most profound.

"How are you doing, Joe? Are you too tired to talk? Should I let you sleep?"

"You're kind to ask. I am tired but would love to hear more about your new struggle. That is, if you don't mind sharing with me."

"I'd love to, Joe."

"Then, please, go right ahead."

She smiled at him and said, "OK. Thanks." She gathered her thoughts. "When I finally opened my heart to God . . . or did he open my heart to him? That is a mystery to me."

"It is a mystery to me as well. It's not meant to be explained, just marveled at, and enjoyed."

"I can do that," she said with a grin. "Anyway, when my heart mysteriously opened to God, the fears that consumed me vanished. They no longer ruled me anymore. But then, the next day, I started noticing things about myself. Things about my mannerisms and nuances concerning the way I related to people . . . things that I did not like. To this day, I'm aware of things in me that are quite disturbing. I thought that when my heart finally opened to God, all the internal struggles would go away. But now there are new struggles, these inner relational struggles that have now surfaced. Can you help me understand? Have I missed something? Is there something else I need to do to stop the struggling? God must be disappointed that I am still struggling."

"No. No. Not at all. In fact, your struggling is a very good sign. The fact that you're wrestling in a new way means that you're aware of areas in your life that are not fully surrendered to God. These relational nuances about yourself, the ones that trouble you, are evidence that your soul is now alive to God. If you felt no internal struggle, I would worry that your change of heart was not real. No, God is not disappointed with you. On the contrary, he is elated that you are now more sensitive to what gets in the way of loving others, loving him."

"Oh wow. That's actually encouraging. How long will these struggles last?"

"They will last as long as you're on the road."

"Oh." She looked around her somewhat befuddled. "What road is that?" she asked.

"The salvation road."

"Oh." Her mind worked to take this in. "So salvation is actually a road?"

"Salvation starts with a door. When the door is opened,

I'm speaking of the door of your heart, then that puts you on the salvation road. That's when the salvation journey begins. You are now on that road, Dalia . . . and I couldn't be happier for you. So many wondrous truths to discover about yourself, about others, about God. The struggle is very real. It's a good sign."

"OK. That sounds exciting but also a bit unnerving. I thought fear would be a thing of the past when I came to know God."

"Your fears no longer dominate you the way they did before. Before you received Christ, you were enslaved to sin and terror brought on by eternal separation. That's not the case anymore. But yes, you will continue to experience fear at times because while your sin has been forgiven, the temptation toward sin is still very real in you. However, it is no longer the deepest reality in you. The Holy Spirit now lives in you and is more powerful than your sin, more powerful than your fears. It's God's work to move you down the salvation road. That's a really good thing. The Father, Son, and Spirit delight in getting their good work in you accomplished." They both gazed at the candelabra near the picture of Maria.

"That's really good to hear," Dalia said as she exhaled. "But what do I do with the struggle?"

"You don't need to do anything with the struggle. You just need to acknowledge it and learn what it means to struggle well."

"Struggle well?"

"Yes, struggle well. Bring your struggles honestly to God. He is not afraid of them. You cannot shock God with your ongoing struggle. He sees it all anyway. He wants you to wrestle honestly with him. When you read the Bible, you'll encounter so many honest strugglers. Their stories will encourage yours. Like I said, you are in very good company, Dalia. So many honest strugglers have gone before you. Believe me when I say that learning to struggle well with God will do your heart a lot of good as you saunter with the Father, Son, and Spirit on the salvation road."

"That has the ring of such good news," Dalia said, a bit flabbergasted.

"That's what the word 'gospel' actually means, 'good news.'"

Dalia's eyes widened with illumination.

"I know, it's a lot to take in. But you'll do fine, more than fine. Remember, it is God who is ultimately in charge. He's in no hurry with you. You don't have to be in a hurry with him, or yourself."

"Thank you," she said, misty-eyed.

Silence ensued.

Joe struggled to speak. "Let's leave it there, shall we?"

"That's good with me, my friend. Is there anything else I can do for you before I go?"

"You've already done so much. I don't know how to thank you for your wonderfully gentle way with me."

"I'm glad you experienced me that way."

She gathered her things into her bag. Then she paused and looked at him. "Do you ever wonder what it's like?"

"I'm not sure what you mean. Can you elaborate?"

"What is beyond the veil of this world?"

"You mean if somehow we could peel it back, what would we see?"

"Yes," she replied.

After a long silence, he said, "I wonder about it all the time."

"One day we'll get to see it, won't we, Joe?"

"I'm banking everything on it, Dalia. It will be a good day indeed."

Her eyes filled with tears. "To be continued, Joe?"

"Absolutely, Dalia. To be continued."

She quietly slipped out the door.

Moments after Dalia had left, Joe could feel the darkness looming all around him. He would have grabbed the bed rails, but his arms were too weak. His heart pounded, and his mind began to race. Dark thoughts like splinters began to pierce his mind. *What good is my life? Have I ever done anything worthwhile? Do people see any good inside of me? Have I ever impacted anyone for the good? Does God see what is good in me? Does he care? God, are you real? Why can't I feel your reassuring presence?* The questions were exhausting. His utter fatigue gave way to sleep. As Joe's eyes closed, he was gently transported.

TWELVE
BEYOND THE VEIL

You'll be given the robes of princes. You'll be
flying on golden wings. You will live in pavilions of splendor.
Be surrounded by beautiful things. So hold on to these
promises. And keep them in your hand. Didn't
anyone ever tell you. This is your land.
- Phil Baggaley, David Clifton, & Ian Blythe,
City of Gold (Album)

W hen Joe opened his eyes, he was on the back of some kind of gloriously winged creature, shimmering with feathers that appeared to be made of an intertwining of silver and gold. *What kind of creature is this?* With much fear and trepidation, he decided to ask, "Excuse me, but are you an angel?"

"I am indeed."

"Oh, that's good to know. I thought I was going a bit

crazy. It's not every day that people get to ride on the back of an angel."

"No, you're not crazy, Joseph. All of this is very real."

Looking at himself, he noticed he was in his young body once more. "Is this finally my entrance into heaven?"

"Not quite yet. But the time is close at hand."

As his eyes came into focus, he was astonished at what he saw. The angel had taken him somewhere out of the earth's atmosphere. The earthly veil was peeled back, and he beheld two rivers, each leading to one of two destinations. One river led to a dark land much like the one where Joe encountered the figure. The other destination led to a bright and glorious city, which reflected costly diamonds and other precious jewels. *A city made of jewels?* The light coming from the city was vibrant and penetrating. Joe looked at the city, and his heart began to yearn, his holy thirst once more ignited.

The angel flew above the rivers in a circular motion, like a hawk riding the wind. Joe noticed there was something strange about the rivers. They didn't seem to be made of water. There were shadowy movements within the rivers that appeared to have bodily form. He stretched his head over the angel's shoulder so he could get a better look. *What are those things in the rivers? Why, those aren't things at all. They look like people, or perhaps souls? Rivers of souls! Each river flowing with souls!*

He heard a cacophony of voices from the souls headed to the dark place, which he presumed was hell. To the bright city, he heard a kind of music that made his heart leap for joy. It was, he was quite sure, the music of heaven.

I've never heard music like that! His heart yearned even more.

Then swiftly, the angel took a nosedive. He was back in the earth's atmosphere again. Joe wrapped his arms around the angel's neck and held on for dear life. They soared through the sky, through clouds, over mountains, into lush green valleys, then down into towns and streets that were familiar to Joe. He was transfixed.

The angel flew low to the ground with its wings spread out wide. He encircled a quaint little house nestled on a small street. The house had a small backyard encircled by a wooden fence. Around the fence line were tomato plants with tomatoes of all different shapes and sizes.

"That's Nonna's house!" Joe exclaimed.

"Yes, Joseph. It's your grandmother's house," came the thundering voice of the angel. He flipped Joe in the air with one strong arch of his back, turned over, and caught him as he was coming down. Joe was now resting on the angel's chest. The winged creature was gliding through the air on his back, with his wings slowly swooping to keep them hovering in the air.

Joe looked into the angel's face, which was not unlike the face of a man with long flowing white hair. His face shone with a fierce brightness.

The angel continued talking. "The Father had his eye on you even when you were a young boy. The Father chose you before you came into being and gave you to his Son, Jesus. He has kept you safe in his love all these years. Do you see, Joseph? You have never been defined by your sin and failures. Even the darkness has never defined you. You chose Jesus, but in fact, God really chose you."

With tears running down his cheeks, Joe was able to say, "What mystery! Thank you so much for reminding me."

"Thank you, Joseph," came the angel's voice.

"You're thanking me?" he said, dumbfounded. "For what?"

"For heeding the call on your life. You would be astonished to know how encouraging your faithfulness has been for those who are like me."

"Really? Oh my goodness. I had no idea. No idea at all!"

The angel smiled. Joe had to shield his eyes from the brightness emanating from his face.

"Would you like to see more?" he said with a gleam in his eye.

"Oh yes, yes, please! I would love to see more!"

"Well then, hang on!" The angel threw out his broad chest, which catapulted Joe into the air. His arms and legs were flailing. The angel turned over, and Joe landed on his back again. He instinctively grabbed on to his neck.

"Here we go!" said the winged creature as he soared straight up into the sky, rotating, rotating, rotating as he picked up speed. He flew past planets and stars and galaxies. *All this that I'm seeing, it defies description. Wonders beyond comprehension!*

"Jesus had a good time making all that you see," said the angel. "It was the Father's pleasure to give his Son the authority to create all of this, the Holy Spirit animated in both of them while it was happening. It was the Holy Spirit who was hovering over creation like a mother eagle hovering over her young. The Spirit still hovers today. The Holy Spirit has been hovering over *you*, Joseph. Do you see? Nothing has ever been at stake. You have been a masterpiece in the making since you came into the world, not primarily for your own pleasure, but for God's. You reflect who they are by how you have been made and remade and remade again."

"Right now, I can't think of anything more wonderful."

"Hold on tight, Joseph. There's more to see."

The angel turned toward the earth again and soared with lightning speed. He soared on the very edge of the earth's atmosphere so Joe could see the curvature of the earth. *Amazing!* A few hours later, the angel came to a slow glide over a place in the northwest United States. He circled a house with a screened-in back porch.

"Wait a minute, I know this place. This is where I lived in Seattle. This is where . . . this is the place where . . ."

"Yes, faithful one, this is where you opened your heart to Jesus Christ." The angel's entire body began to shiver with joy as he spoke the Lord's name. "There was a big party in heaven that day. It never gets old seeing human souls opening their hearts to Jesus for the first time. The good news is made fresh with every new soul that opens up to him."

The tears were now streaming again. "It's a special place. No doubt about it. I had no idea what was in store for me. But looking back on it now, seeing this place again, I couldn't be more grateful."

"You were dead and were made alive in the depths of your being." Now the angel hovered low to the ground so they were almost eye level to the back porch.

"Can anyone see us?"

"No. No one can."

"Are we in a vision, in liminal space?"

"No. We are in the present, but no one can see us."

Joe gazed at the house. "I remember weeping on that porch. Tears of loneliness and isolation. I experienced an anguish I had never known."

"The fallenness in you was great back then."

"It reached a tipping point on that porch. I suppose the anguish was necessary. I don't think I could have heard the living truth if I hadn't first experienced the anguish. In that sense, I am deeply grateful for the anguish. It led me to God."

The angels wings were swooping up and down so smoothly they were hardly making a sound. They remained still in the air. "Those are Spirit-led words, Joseph."

"Yes, yes. I suppose they are. They don't make any sense without him."

"Have you seen enough of this place?" said the angel in a gentle voice.

"I think so. Thank you so much for bringing me here."

"They wanted you to remember."

Joe brought his face close to the angel's ear. "Who?"

"The Father, Son, and Holy Spirit. They wanted you to remember the day Jesus ransomed your soul from the darkness of sin and brought you into their circle of holy love."

Misty-eyed, Joe replied, "It's so good to remember. I hope I never forget."

"I doubt you ever shall, Joseph. The salvation of the Lord is celebrated throughout all of eternity. The uniqueness of how he saves each human soul is also celebrated."

"Now, why doesn't that surprise me," Joe said as they continued to hover.

"Onward?" the angel said.

"Onward."

Gently, the strong angel elevated into the sky as the sun was just rising. Joe had relaxed his grip and sat back on his knees placing his hands on his hips. *Hey, I'm starting to get the hang of this.*

Just then the angel rocked left then right.

"Whoa!" screamed Joe as he almost fell off the winged creature.

"Ha, ha!" The angel's laugh reverberated in the air.

"Oh I see how it is! I didn't realize angels had a sense of humor," Joe said, now tightly holding the angel's neck again.

"Well, now you know, Joseph!"

"How great! I continue to discover new things in these mysterious encounters."

"There's so much more to discover. Discoveries that continue throughout all eternity."

"I can't wait."

"Onward?" the angel said again.

"Yes, onward!" Joe said, raising his right arm as if going into battle.

The angel swiftly navigated his way through valleys and stretches of mountain peaks. A few hours passed. He came to hover over a house that was familiar to Joe. "That's Patrick and Sonya's house!" A deep yearning rose in his heart. "They mean so much to me!"

Just then, Patrick and Sonya came walking out the front door with their two kids in tow. "It looks like they're taking the kids to the bus stop." He couldn't take his eyes off them.

"You loved them well, Joseph."

"Really? I sure hope so. My gosh, I miss them so much. Letting them go is harder than I could've imagined."

"They are in good hands, dear one. One day you will understand."

"I wish that day was now." His heart now ached with a familiar pain. "I will do my best to leave them in the Lord's hands."

"Such good words, Joseph."

They hovered in silence for a while and watched as Patrick and Sonya hugged their kids before they boarded the school bus.

Joe was doing his best to hold it together. "I think it is best to go now," he said to the angel, fighting back the tears.

Without a word, the strong angel lifted into the morning sky, moving through cornfields, canyons, and cities. Several hours later, the angel came to an ice rink in southern New Hampshire.

"There's Anna and Sam!" He looked closer. "That's my granddaughter figure skating on the ice!" *Maybe one day she'll get to ice skate with my mother. Wouldn't that be a sight to see.*

As the tears trickled down his face, he wondered what it would be like to hold his granddaughter in his arms again. Then his mind went to his daughter. "Anna was such a tiny thing when she was born. Now, look at her. All grown up and a mom herself. Oh, how I have missed her." He began to quietly sob.

"Put your hands around my neck, Joseph," said the winged creature. With hardly any disruption, the angel placed his wings at his sides and turned over cradling Joe against his chest, enveloping him in his arms. His wings kept them hovering in the air. He whispered into his ear, "You've done so well, Joseph. You have done so well." The angel let him sob until Joe became quiet.

Joe took another glance at his granddaughter skating timidly on the ice rink. "Have you seen anything more beautiful?"

"She is beautiful. There is no doubt. She's in good hands too. Anna and Sam are strong and wise parents. They will lead her well."

"She looks so much like her mother." With the familiar ache swelling in his chest, he repeated what he said about Patrick and Sonya. "I will do my best to leave them all in the hands of our good, good God . . . as best as I know how."

They stayed for a little while longer until the angel said, "Shall we go, Joseph?"

"Okay. Yes. We can go now."

Once Joe was on his back again, the angel soared smoothly and swiftly into the early afternoon sun, over lakes and neighborhoods. After several hours, the angel came to hover over a place in North Carolina, a place Joe knew only too well. It was his nursing home. The angel gently flipped Joe in the air and turned over so Joe came to rest on the angel's chest once again. He wrapped his strong arms around him. Then he gently turned over, facing down, so that Joe was suspended in midair hanging downward. The angel wrapped his wings around Joe and began to slowly descend.

It's like lying in a shimmering hammock! As he lay nestled in the soft and strong wings of the angel, Joe gazed into his dazzling face. "You're amazing," he said. "I can't thank you enough."

"Thank you, Joseph, for allowing me to take you on this small journey."

"There was nothing small about it."

The angel's face beamed, and Joe saw an expression on his face that could only be described as fierce joy. The strong angel took in a deep breath and then exhaled. As he did so, a wonderfully warm sensation gently swept over Joe. He closed his eyes in satisfaction. When he opened his eyes, the angel was gone, and he was back in his hospital bed at Bright Star nursing home.

THIRTEEN
THE LAST DOOR

Come to me, all you who are weary and burdened,
and I will give you rest. Take my yoke upon you and learn
from me, for I am gentle and humble in heart,
and you will find rest for your souls.
- Matthew 11:28–29, NIV

As Joe lay there in his hospital bed, he could tell that his body had become significantly weaker. He tried to call out for someone but could not speak. His breathing became shallow. His eyes could no longer focus as they once did. Joe knew that he was nearing the threshold, and as his body weakened, his spirit gained strength.

He remained this way for a couple of days. He could no longer eat or drink. However, he found to his surprise that he could still think and he could still hear. Much of the time was used to pray, not for himself but for those he knew and loved.

He prayed for his two adult children, Pat and Anna, and their families. He knew they would be struggling with his imminent death. He also knew that his death would also be a great relief to them. Together, they had shouldered the burden of caring for him. They did not like watching him suffer.

Yet, Pat and Anna, along with their spouses, Sonya and Sam, never placed the burden of their grief on him. It was something they held quietly, in a way that did not hide their grief, but also in a way that did not make it the point.

Joe instinctively knew that while they were dealing with anticipatory grief, they also were swelling with anticipatory joy for what life would be like for Joe when he finally crossed over the threshold into heaven.

He also prayed for Dalia, asking the Lord to strengthen her faith, that she might find a small community where she could learn to be her God-designed self. She would need other Christians to walk with her, and Joe knew God would provide in his own way.

Joe was aware of someone coming into the room. "Hello, my dear friend," said the voice quietly.

It's Dalia.

Joe could sense that she was kneeling near his bedside. He could hear her quietly weeping. "Joe," she said, "I'm going to take a mouth swab and dip it in water just so I can moisten your mouth. It's just a little sponge on the end of a small stick. I promise it won't hurt you. It's just that your mouth is extremely dry since you can no longer breathe out of your nose. It should be of some help to you." She gently swabbed Joe's lips, the inside of his cheeks, and the tip of his tongue.

How in tune she is with the needs of the dying.

He tried to focus his eyes again so he could see her. Surprisingly, they did focus now in a different way. The thin veil between this world and the next slowly began to dissipate. He could see Dalia, sitting close to him, her eyes moist with tears and a warm smile on her face.

She went over to the candelabra still sitting on a table near Maria's picture. She pulled out a lighter and lit each candle. Then she came back and knelt by his side. "I received permission to light these candles. Since you are not wearing oxygen anymore, there is no danger of an explosion." She touched his arm gently. "I don't know if you can see them, Joe, but I hope you can."

I can see them, my friend. How beautiful they are! Joe wished she could hear him as his heart swelled with gratitude for her.

Joe became aware of a door in the corner of the room. This particular door seemed out of place. It had thick green vines growing around the frame on the left side, with golden leaves adorning the frame on the right side. The inner frame of the door consisted of wood from a large tree from which everything seemed to be growing. There were small red flowers speckled through the dark green and gold leaves. A bright light was shining into Joe's room from the other side of the door. As Joe looked closer, he could see that the vines were, very slightly, expanding and contracting.

A living door? He attempted to speak again but to no avail. His vocal cords were too weak. All he could let out was a soft moan.

Dalia leaned forward and put her hand on his shoulder.

"I'm here, Joe. I'm right here. Your children are on the way. I was able to speak to them, to let them know that you were . . . that you were . . ." She struggled to finish the sentence "that you were dying."

He so badly wanted to calm her fears but still could not speak. He wanted to reassure her that dying meant the beginning of a new kind of life for him, a vibrant life that defied description. *She knows where I'm going. Yet, how hard it is to leave her!*

His thoughts went to his children. His soul throbbed with the pain of leaving them. Yet, he also had hope. *Whether they make it in time or not, I know I will see them again. They know Jesus and he knows them. For those destined for heaven, there are no final goodbyes.*

"I need to shift your body a little, Joe. Just to keep you from getting bed sores." She gently shifted Joe's body in the hospital bed so he was now lying on his right side.

He was fortunate to now be facing this new, strange door. He was spellbound by the sight of it. As he focused his gaze on the door, he saw several people walk through it into his room.

First to come through was Nonna, adorned in the same blue and teal dress. She whispered his name as she looked at him with fondness. "My dear, dear Joseph, the time has come. The time has finally come. No more sinful relating. Nothing to keep our hearts hidden from each other! Only relational love to be expressed for all eternity!"

His heart quivered as she spoke these words. Although he still could not move. His eyes remained fixated on her.

The next person to walk through was Job. He gave Joe's grandmother a warm embrace. He gazed at Joe with that familiar kind yet wild look. "Joseph, are you up for another adventure? No more anguish. No more internal fist. Nothing to get in the way of relationship with God, relationship with others. No more internal battle to fight my friend. The greatest adventure is now upon you!"

Joe's heart expanded with such a great yearning at these words. Yet, still he was not able to move his body even though he tried with all his might.

The third person to come through the door was Carissa. She seemed to glide effortlessly as she came through the door. Taking Nonna and Job by the arms, she exclaimed exuberantly, "JT! You've waited a long time for this. Now is the time to be happy with the happiness of God! Now is the time to join the eternal dance!"

He wanted to laugh and leap for joy but still could not move. Although, he felt the exuberance building in his spirit.

Then John stepped through the door. The affection and kindness communicated through his smile warmed Joe's heart to the core. He took his time placing his hands on each person's face and looking each of them deeply in the eyes, first Nonna, then Job, and finally Carissa.

He's acknowledging their personhood and uniqueness. What a good man!

He then turned to Joe and said, "The personification of Love, Grace, and Fellowship await you, my lad. The community of love at the center of all things! Yours is an inimitable invitation signed and sealed by the Father, his Son Jesus Christ, and the Holy Spirit! They have been anticipating this moment for a long time, since you came into existence in your mother's womb. Now the time is upon you!"

Joseph's heart was breaking, but not with pain. His heart was breaking with love. No more need to imagine, no more need to envision. He was about to enter reality, the deepest kind.

The next person who waltzed through the door was an utter surprise to Joe. He was a Black man, tall and lean, with quiet muscles rippling underneath his skin. He was dressed in a short-sleeve V-neck shirt and long pants. His clothes appeared to be made out of some sort of silver weave and flickered from the refraction of light. He stretched out his long arms toward the other visitors, and they all embraced in one large circle, jumping up and down at the same time.

After this he turned to Joe and, with joyful tears in his eyes, exclaimed, "Joseph, Joseph, Joseph. My dear brother Joseph! How can I possible thank you for loving my granddaughter!" He put his right hand over his heart and continued, "You couldn't have given me a better gift! I'm looking forward to sharing eternity with you. It's going to be such a good time!"

Oh my goodness! Dalia's grandfather! My heart is brimming with joy! I so look forward to getting to know him!

He tried reaching out to touch him but could not, now more keenly aware of the paradox of growing weaker in body and stronger in spirit. *It's so strange, but it's true. I know I am dying, but I have never felt more alive!*

His heart could not have been prepared for what happened next. Yet, at the same time, Joe was hoping against hope that he would see her walk through the last door. There she was, Maria. She strolled through the door with tears of joy streaming down her face. It startled Joe to see her again in her young body. Her dark brown hair caressing her shoulders. Her olive skin restored to its natural beauty. Her dark purple, sequin dress refracting different colors as it caught the sunlight, while earthly and heavenly dimensions subtly commingled in supernatural pleasure. She approached the others and kissed each of them on the cheek.

Affectionately then, she turned to Joe. The look on her face said it all. It was a look so deep with meaning, a look so full of knowing, a look so energized with life, words were useless to add anything to what was being communicated between them. At that moment, Joe knew. She was fine. She was more than fine. All was well with her, body and soul. At the knowledge of this, the heaviness that Joe carried in his soul instantly vanished.

They all stood there for a few more minutes talking to each other, laughing, waiting, and gazing at Joe with a look of true happiness in their eyes. Then each one of them, in the same order they came into the room, one by one started to walk back through the living door, the *last* door.

Joe watched the procession and for a moment was concerned that his time had not yet come. All of a sudden, Joe began to hear singing. It was a pure and beautiful voice. At first, he wondered if the singing was coming from the other side of the door. It wasn't. The music was coming from his room. It was Dalia. She was singing a song in a most wonderfully gentle way:

Holy, holy, holy! Lord God Almighty!
Early in the morning our song shall rise to thee.
Holy, holy, holy! merciful and mighty!
God in three persons, blessed Trinity!

Holy, holy, holy! all the saints adore thee,
Casting down their golden crowns around the glassy sea.
Cherubim and Seraphim falling down before thee,
Which wert and art and evermore shall be.

Holy, holy, holy! though the darkness hide thee,

Though the eye of sinful man thy glory may not see,
Only thou art holy, there is none beside thee,
Perfect in power, in love, and purity.

Holy, holy, holy! Lord God Almighty!
All thy works shall praise thy name in earth and sky and sea.
Holy, holy, holy! merciful and mighty!
God in three persons, blessed Trinity

Joe was mesmerized. *Oh my . . . the singing . . . and those words! How often have I sung that song. Yet now, hearing Dalia singing. It seems so fresh to me!*

His heart was bursting with praise! He glanced over at Dalia's grandfather who had not yet walked back through the last door. He had his arms raised, and tears were trickling down his face. He mouthed the words as Dalia was singing.

After finishing the song, Dalia said to Joe tenderly, "That was one of my grandfather's favorites. He used to quietly sing it all the time. It never had any meaning for me, until now, Joe. I'm going to miss you, my friend. But I will go on without you. I will walk, maybe stumble at times, down the salvation road, until we see each other again."

After she said these words, Dalia could not contain her mixture of grief and joy and started sobbing, placing her face in her hands. Joe could see her grandfather watching and listening. He was weeping also.

Those aren't tears of grief in his eyes. Those are tears of joy!

Her grandfather slowly turned, taking one last glance at Joe, and made his way back through the door. Maria was the only one left. Extending both of her arms, with her hands outstretched, she gazed at Joe and said in a powerful voice, "It's time!"

Quietly then, Joe breathed his last breath on earth . . . and then . . . effortlessly breathed his first breath on the threshold of heaven. His spirit had separated from his withered body. He stood straight and tall in his young, new, vibrant heavenly body. He looked himself up and down, utterly amazed. Then he looked at Maria, embraced her, and then firmly took her hand. Joe walked with her toward the door. As he reached the threshold of the last door, Joe took one more glance back at Dalia. He whispered one last thing to her.

"To be continued, my friend."

He knew she couldn't hear him . . . or could she? He really didn't know . . . but hoped so.

Then, Joseph Rafael Tropea walked over the threshold of the last door. The moment he stepped in, his eyes widened, and he gasped. There standing before him was the one person he had longed to see ever since his conversion in Seattle on that rainy winter night. Before him in that moment, as Joe gazed into the most tender and forgiving eyes he had ever encountered, he finally understood. All his earthly life, Joe had seen through a glass dimly. Now, finally, he saw face-to-face. As he collapsed into the arms of Jesus, the nail-scarred hands enveloped him in a welcoming embrace. "Well done, Joseph. Well done. Now enter into your happiness and rest."

Joe inhaled deeply as if to take the words into his very being. As Joe gazed into the face of the greatest lover of his soul, his holy thirst was wholly satisfied.

Just then a man came up to him. It was the homeless man Joe encountered so many years ago in Manhattan. Now, young, vibrant, and alive, he pulled Joe in close, embraced him, kissed him on both cheeks, and with tears in his eyes looked him square in the face. "Those words I said to you on the streets of New York were true. But they were incomplete. All fears are indeed rooted in the fear of death. Yet, it is also true that every moment of real joy is rooted in the deepest joy of all, the joy that can only be discovered on the salvation road. You've struggled well, Joseph. Now you are finally home."

Instinctively, they looked at Jesus who was standing right there, in the flesh. Laying their heads on his chest, they wrapped their arms around his waist and whispered together, "Thank you, dear Lord. Thank you."

AUTHOR'S NOTE

This book emerged out of a dark night of the soul. I was in my living room lamenting the felt absence of God and wondering, like the beloved in the Song of Solomon, where the lover of my soul had gone (Song of Solomon 5:6). I take comfort in the fact that several well-known Christians struggled with the same thing. People like Mother Teresa, who labored fifty years with the poor in Calcutta, the famous hymn writer William Cowper, the great Puritan preacher Charles Spurgeon, the compassionate priest and writer Henri Nouwen, my mentor Dr. Larry Crabb, not to mention Jesus, who quoted Psalm 22 while hanging on the cross, "My God, my God, why have you forsaken me?"

It's important to remember that Jesus said he would be with us always. This is an unequivocal guarantee for those who know him. However, while he did say he would always be with us, he did *not* say we would always feel his presence. In fact, God hides himself at times in order to do a more profound work in our souls (Isaiah 45:15).

The hidden blessing of not being aware of God's

presence is that it teaches us to live with our holy thirst. In fact, our thirst for God intensifies as we mature and sustains us in a way his felt presence can't.

It is the privilege of those who desire to walk closely with him. God respects us by, at times, withdrawing a sense of his presence and intensifying our longing for what only heaven can provide, calling us to live by faith rather than by mere feelings (Hebrews 11). As an older man, now the age of sixty-two, I understand the truth of this a bit more and, in my better moments, feel deeply trusted by God that he would allow me to rest in his love and live out of his love, even when I don't feel it.

The book took shape as I wrote it. I did not have an outline beforehand. Many of the writers who have influenced me wrote the same way, my mentor, Larry Crabb, being one of them. I don't claim that this is the only way to write or even the better way to write. I do think it is best to think about our own wiring and seek to be true to how God has fashioned us. The word "organic" was important to me as I wrote. I wanted the novel to emerge naturally out of me. For whatever reason, I believe it kept me dependent on the Holy Spirit. There were days when all I could manage to write was one sentence. There were other days I was able to write much more.

I did have in mind a story that included heaven. I think because heaven is rarely talked about even in Christian circles. As a hospice chaplain, it's hard to avoid thinking about heaven or hell for that matter. Eternity is constantly before me as I stand at the threshold with people. I'm not saying that eternity should dominate all of our thinking all of the time. We need to live in the here and now, finding God in our ordinary lives, in our present relationships. Yet, I do strongly believe that eternity should deeply shape our thinking and our living. I don't agree with the common adage that those who are heavenly minded are no earthly good. I have found the opposite to be true. To embrace my final destination, to remember the city God has prepared, brings me a deep sense of hope and meaning for how I live my life in the present. Jesus himself told us to store up our treasure in heaven where thieves could not steal, nor moths, nor rust, destroy. For where our treasure is, there our hearts would be also (Matthew 6). Perhaps, we should take him at his word.

Shortly before he died, Larry wrote a brief letter to me in response to one of mine. Among other things, I had written him about my longing for heaven. I keep his letter framed on my desk. I offer his words to you:

> Hi friend. Your note encouraged me. I don't say that out of mere courtesy. I've never felt my unsatisfied desires more fully and have never depended more strongly on the hope, the twin hope, that he is doing a good work in me even as I fail and struggle and that the Day of Eternal Satisfaction is coming. Press on, Anthony. We journey together on this cross narrow road. - Larry

May we struggle well with God, keeping our final destination in mind. For those who know him, heaven is the place where life truly begins.

The best is yet to come.

- Anthony J. Vartuli

ACKNOWLEDGMENTS

I wish there were more room to acknowledge all the people who have influenced my journey with God over the years. The list is long. For those who have traveled with me, you know who you are.

To founder, CEO, and developmental editor at Tandem services, Jennifer Crosswhite as well as editor Katy Schlomach at Tandem services: Your input made this a much better book. I'm very grateful to you both.

To Jean Fast: Thank you for reading my manuscript and giving me such thoughtful feedback. It is so good to travel with you in our small group.

To Rich Pilon: Fellow pastor and dear friend. Your initial reading of my manuscript gave me courage to keep writing. I'm so glad that God has allowed our lives to intersect. I'm very grateful for you, brother.

To my daughter, Giovanna: Thanks for designing my book cover, reading my manuscript, and offering feedback. It was so helpful.

To Eric Broadbent: A friend who mentored me when I was a young Christian. Thank you for nurturing my thirst for God.

To Larry Crabb: A long time mentor who helped me think about the Bible relationally.

To Tom Board: I appreciate your curiosity about my desire to write. It helped to keep me going.

To Kent and Karla Denlinger, founders of Soul Signature Ministries: You've helped shape my thinking and my relating. Thank you for being friends all these years.

To my children and their spouses: Michael and Kendra Vartuli (and little Giana), Giovanna Vartuli, Julia and Cy Bryan. Suffice to say, my affection for each of you runs very deep. As your father (and father-in-law) I couldn't be more proud.

Finally, to my wife of thirty-two years, Diane. Your support for this project, from beginning to end, has been so deeply encouraging. Your reading of my manuscript (twice) really challenged me. By doing so this book is so much better. You not only speak Christ with your words. You speak Christ with your life. My gratitude for you runs far deeper than I can express. Thank you, honey. We journey together toward home.

ABOUT THE AUTHOR

Anthony has been in ministry for 38 years in various capacities: pastor, teacher, spiritual director, and hospice chaplain. He has walked alongside many people, some who are celebrating, others who are suffering. He has a Master of Theology Degree from Dallas Theological Seminary, a Master of Arts in Biblical Counseling Degree from Colorado Christian University, and a Doctor of Ministry Degree in Spiritual Formation and Leadership from Gordon-Conwell Theological Seminary. He is currently an ordained chaplain with The Christian & Missionary Alliance. He resides in Colorado with his wife, Diane. Together they have three adult children and one grandchild.

Their website is sojournwayministries.org